SECOND CHANCE RANCHER

BY
PATRICIA THAYER

First Published in Great Britain 2016
By Mills & Boon, an imprint of HarperCollins*Publishers*
1 London Bridge Street, London, SE1 9GF

© 2016 Patricia Wright

ISBN: 978-0-263-92022-2

23-0916

Our policy is to use papers that are natural, renewable and recyclable products and made from wood grown in sustainable forests. The logging and manufacturing processes conform to the legal environmental regulations of the country of origin.

Printed and bound in Spain
by CPI, Barcelona

Patricia Thayer was born and raised in Muncie, Indiana, the second in a family of eight children. She attended Ball State University before heading west, where she has called Southern California home for many years. There she's been a member of the Orange County Chapter of RWA. It's a sisterhood like no other.

When not working on a story, she might be found traveling the United States and Europe, taking in the scenery and doing story research while enjoying time with her husband, Steve. Together, they have three grown sons and four grandsons and one granddaughter, whom Patricia calls her own true-life heroes.

To my readers who have faithfully read me
over the years. You are the reason this story
is my 50th book for Harlequin.

And always to Steve.
My dad might have been my first hero,
but you are my forever hero.
Love you.

Chapter One

Laurel Quinn drove the all-terrain vehicle over the rough pasture at the Bucking Q Ranch. The ATV was ideal for getting around in the hilly pastureland. In the Colorado winters, the ranch hands had to switch to snowmobiles to find lost cattle. Today, she wasn't looking for lost calves, but for one runaway stallion. Gripping the steering wheel tighter, she flew over a rise but still kept an eye peeled for the honey-brown-colored quarter horse.

Sadly, she seemed to have trouble keeping a male, no matter what the species. Right now, though, she had to focus all her attention on the valuable horse, Capture the Wind.

A stallion was always harder to train, and to keep confined, especially when a mare was in season. And this guy was double the trouble. She'd been thinking about gelding the golden-brown bay if he kept escaping. It was a good thing he'd made some money for his stud service. That was the only thing that saved his sorry hide. She was anxious to see his first foals. Then his price would go up.

She drove through a group of aspen trees and looked upward at the cloud-speckled sky above the familiar green and brown hues of the Rocky Mountains. Off in the distance were the familiar granite peaks of the Maroon Bell. She loved springtime on the ranch. Nature came to life with new growth and new births. Soon, her newly found twin sister, Brooke, and her husband, neighboring rancher Trent Landry, would be having their first child. A son. They were going to name him Christopher after Trent's brother, who'd died in a tragic accident years ago. Although a little envious, she was happy for her sister.

Off in the distance, Laurel spotted the downed fence and slowed the ATV. With a curse, she reached for her cell phone and called the Bucking Q barn. This job was going to be more difficult than she thought. Then she realized this was a border fence. Her horse was now on Rawlins property.

The ranch foreman answered, "Chet Bradshaw."

"Hey, Chet, it's Laurel. Looks like Wind got over the fence in the south pasture. The posts are rotted out, so could you send out a couple of the guys to repair them? It's about a mile south of Rainbow Canyon."

"Wait for me. I'll bring Billy along because I don't want you tangling with the stallion alone."

She wasn't as worried about the horse as the neighbors. "First, I've got to find him." She heard a loud whinny off in the distance. "Gotta go."

She tossed her phone on the seat, then eased her vehicle through the opening in the fence. She didn't think about her trespassing onto Rawlins land, or the fact that the last person she wanted to run into was Kase. She'd known for a while that the prodigal son had returned home.

Wind whinnied again, and she shot off toward the corral, not knowing if the stallion was injured or trapped or what. All she knew was she had to get to her horse. Her future depended on this animal.

At one time, she'd known the Rawlins Horse Ranch as well as her dad's ranch. Gus Rawlins had taught her nearly everything she knew about equines. Then that day ten years ago she'd had her heart broken by Kase… She shook away the memory. Those days were long gone.

She drove over the uneven ground, praying Wind hadn't been hurt or caused any more trouble. Maybe if she were lucky, she'd find him before anyone discovered her on the property.

She heard the familiar whinny again. She drove over the rise to see a corral and there was her horse, his black mane and tail flying as he pranced around the arena as if he owned the place.

Then she turned her attention to another horse. A glistening chestnut…mare. Oh, no.

She hit the gas pedal and raced down the hill, hoping to prevent what she knew was about to happen. She stopped at the broken boards of the fence, grabbed Wind's lead rope off the seat and climbed through the splintered wood. She yelled and waved her arms, but nothing could stop the crazed stallion. Wind raised up on his hind legs and quickly mounted the willing mare. Laurel stuck her fingers in her mouth and let go of a loud whistle as if that would stop this act of nature. Not. "Damn!"

All she could do was stand back out of the way. There was no finesse about animals mating. They were loud and sometimes brutal as the powerful stallion's forelegs gripped the mare's sides and he drove into her body several times.

Once Wind finished, he dropped back from the other horse. He threw his head back and released a soft whinny, then sauntered over toward her as if he had just taken a stroll in the park.

She attached the lead rope to Wind's halter. He blew out a loud breath. "*Now* you come to me."

"It seemed he was a little busy before."

Laurel swung around to see the tall, handsome man. His sandy-brown hair under his black cowboy hat was shorter than she remembered, but his deep-set gray eyes could still mesmerize her. The worst thing possible, Kase Rawlins could still make her heart race. She cursed under her breath.

"Kase? What are you doing here?"

He folded his large arms over his chest. "I live here." He walked over to the mare, examined her quickly, took hold of the horse's halter and walked her to one of the ranch hands. Once the mare was in the barn, he came back to her. With a nod toward her stallion, he said, "I take it this guy belongs to you."

Laurel nodded, unable to make eye contact. It had been ten years since her first love took off for college and never came back. "This is Capture the Wind. I'm so sorry about what happened. He got away from my handler. I came after him…but not in time."

"You should be sorry." He nodded toward the horse headed through the barn door. "We had plans to breed Honor's Promise. Even paid the stud fee."

She definitely didn't have the money to repay him right now. "Well, I didn't plan this, either. And if it's any consolation, Wind is registered, and he gets a substantial stud fee." Which was a stretch, since he hadn't sired any foals. Yet. She'd had him only a few months, but her mare, Starr Gazer, her best cutter, was pregnant.

He blinked those steel-gray eyes at her. "You don't expect me to pay for what just happened here."

She tossed her long braid over her shoulder and jammed her hands on her hips. "Of course not, but don't insult Wind like he's some mongrel horse that runs wild."

Kase couldn't believe Laurel Quinn would show up here of all places. His gaze couldn't help but wander over the girl he once knew. It seemed like a million years ago when he was young and arrogant. There was still that deep fire in her green eyes. Damn, if it didn't have him thinking about all the times they'd been together. Also their last argument before he'd left Hidden Springs.

Laurel had been only eighteen then. She might still have that long braid, but she definitely was a woman now. His gaze moved over her body, full breasts and long, shapely legs. He had no business thinking about her, or any woman, right now.

"I have no clue to the bloodline of this stallion."

"Well, believe me, he has an impressive pedigree."

"Too bad he doesn't have any manners."

Kase eyed the magnificent stallion. At least sixteen hands, he had a rich golden-brown coat and black mane and tail. And was cocky as hell. This might be a good thing. Of course, he wasn't the expert. That would be his dad.

The large animal danced sideways, but Laurel managed to hang on to the lead rope. He would offer to help her with the horse, but he knew she'd turn him down.

"I'll pay for any damages to the fence."

"Good, I'll send you a bill." He'd planned to repair the rotted wood that had been neglected the past few years. There had been several things around here that needed attention. Now that he had the time, he planned to get to them. "You still live at home?"

She straightened. "I live *at* the ranch. I have an apartment over the garage. I breed and train horses there, so being close to my horses is important." She flashed those big green eyes at him. "So how long are you staying?"

He hesitated, not sure how much he wanted to tell her. "Not sure... I need to help Dad with the ranch." Maybe by then, he'd figure out what to do with his life and handle the problems he'd left back in the city.

He saw Laurel's surprise. There had been a time when he'd sworn he would never set foot on this ranch again. He was going to be a big-time lawyer and make a name for himself. Well, that dream had cost him dearly, and it'd cost Addy even more.

"But I thought… Aren't you practicing law in Denver?"

"Not at the moment. I'm taking some time off."

She glanced around. "Is Gus okay?"

In a town the size of Hidden Springs, there weren't many secrets. "He needs hip surgery. So he will be out of commission for a while. I came back to stay and help out."

He couldn't stop watching as she stroked the stallion. This wild beast had suddenly become docile with her touch. He remembered those hands on him… His attention went to her mouth. At eighteen she hadn't been experienced with anything but horses. Yet her innocent kisses had turned him inside out.

He'd heard at the local diner that she'd nearly gotten married a few months back. Then the bridegroom had run off with her heart and the family's money.

"Daddy! Daddy!"

Kase turned to see his father, Gus, bracing his four-year-old daughter, Addison, on the middle rung of the corral fence. Addy had sunny-yellow hair that lay in ringlets against her tiny shoulders. Several curls had escaped, probably because he couldn't fasten the clips correctly. Her blue-gray eyes were wide with excitement, and her big smile melted his heart. She'd been wearing jeans, T-shirts and new cowboy boots since they'd arrived home. She told him she was a cowgirl now.

"Hey, sweetie. What are you doing out here?"

"Papa said I could come out if I stayed out of the way."

He looked at his dad. The cagey old guy had a grin on his weathered face. "We saw you had company and we wanted to come out and say hi. Didn't we, sweet pea?"

His daughter's head bobbed up and down. "And to see the pretty horsey."

He wasn't sure if he was ready for this introduction, but he might as well get it over with. "That's Capture the Wind, sweetie."

Addy's attention went to Laurel. "Who's the lady, Daddy?"

He glanced over his shoulder to see Laurel's surprised look. "This is Laurel Quinn, our neighbor and the owner of the horse. Laurel, this is my daughter, Addison Marie Rawlins."

Addy waved. "Hi, Laurel. I'm four years old."

"Hi, Addy." Laurel finally smiled back. "I'm twenty-eight."

"Laurel, can I pet your horsey?"

Gus nodded toward Wind. "I wouldn't mind a closer look at that animal myself."

Laurel looked at Kase, and at his nod she tugged on the reins and started across the corral. "You stay right there and I'll bring him to you." Then she said to the stallion, "Mind your manners."

Kase watched Laurel's movements as she walked the large animal across the corral. She matched the spirited animal with her long strides. No doubt she was the boss and Wind was doing her bidding. He followed her like a gentle lamb.

Of course, he was more interested in the woman. Captivated by those long legs and full hips encased in a pair of faded jeans. She still wore the standard cowboy uniform, manure-caked boots and that old battered straw cowboy hat. She was a working cowgirl, and everything he'd never wanted. Then why did she still get to him?

Laurel was nervous. A few months ago, she'd heard that Kase was back in town. She thought it was for only a short visit. It was hard to believe the big-time Denver lawyer had moved his entire family back here. No sign of his wife—maybe she'd stayed in Denver.

She put on a smile and looked at Gus. "Hi, Gus."

"Hey there, Laurel. Haven't seen you in a long time."

She nodded. "A few years."

"You're still as pretty as a picture, and I hear good things about you and your horses."

"Thank you. This guy might get me to change my mind." She patted Wind's neck. "So sorry about what happened. I can guarantee if your mare ends up pregnant, you won't be disappointed. If so, I'll buy the foal."

"Whoa, darlin', let's wait and see what the outcome of today is first," Kase said.

"Papa, is the horsey going to have a baby?"

"We'll see."

The girl clapped her hands. "I hope so."

Addy reached out and petted Wind. "Your horsey is pretty."

"Well, that's the only thing saving him right now. But he's still in trouble because he ran off and broke down a fence."

"Are you gonna put him in a time-out?"

She smiled. "I should, but I'm not sure he'll understand that he did anything wrong. Horses are different from people."

Addy smiled. "I'm glad because Wind is a good horsey and he's soft." The horse bobbed his head as if to agree. The girl continued to stroke the animal without fear. "Papa Gus says you should never treat animals bad."

The child's blue eyes were so expressive. "Do you have any little girls that I can play with?"

Laurel felt a pang of envy and avoided making eye contact with Kase. "No, I don't have any children."

"Oh." Her lower lip came out in a pout. "I got twin Bitty Baby dolls for my birthday. You want to see them?"

She started to decline when Kase stepped in and said, "Laurel can't stay today. She has to take her horse back home. Maybe another time."

She didn't like anyone answering for her. Just then she saw Chet riding over the rise toward them. "Seems I'm not so busy after all. I'll come see your dollies."

"Yeah!" Addy cried.

She avoided looking at Kase but could feel his disdain. "Let me send Wind home with Chet." She led her horse through the downed fence and handed the reins to the foreman. "Hey, Chet."

The young man smiled atop his big black gelding. "So you caught the bad boy."

"Not before he did the damage, and I'm not talking about the fence." She told him about the mare and Chet laughed.

"It's not funny," she argued, but found herself smiling, too. What choice did she have? It had been the way her life had been going lately. Now she was here with the once love of her life.

Chet looked up and studied the threesome at the fence. "Is that Kase Rawlins?"

Laurel avoided eye contact. "Yeah, and his little girl."

The ranch foreman frowned. "Do you think it's a good idea that you're staying?"

Chet was in his midthirties, and he'd been around the Bucking Q since he was a teenager, as far back as when Kase had left. "I appreciate your concern, Chet, but I'm a big girl. So do me a favor, and take Wind back to the barn, and I'll be home in an hour."

She waved and headed back toward the man who'd walked out of her life without a second glance. So why was she putting herself through this again? Good question. Even after all these years, she couldn't think of an answer when it came to Kase Rawlins.

Chapter Two

Questioning her lack of common sense, Laurel followed Addy into the brightly painted lavender bedroom. The centerpiece was a glossy white canopy covered with a floral comforter and lined with stuffed animals.

She smiled at the perfect little-girl's room. And she didn't need to be here. She didn't need to be reminded of everything she didn't have in her life. A home and family of her own. One of the main reasons she wanted to marry last fall, even if she'd chosen the wrong man. A sudden thought popped into her head. Where was this child's mother?

"This is Bobby. Her name is Bonnie," Addy said as she pointed to the two baby dolls sitting on the windowsill.

Laurel sat down beside the child. "Oh, they're so precious." She looked at Addy. "Could I hold one?"

With Addy's enthusiastic nod, Laurel carefully picked up Bobby and cuddled the doll close. "He looks like a real baby."

A pleased-looking Addy followed Laurel's example and reached for the other doll. "I pretend Bobby is my little brother and Bonnie is my sister so I won't be all by myself." The light went out of her eyes that were so much like her father's. "'Cause sometimes I get scared."

Laurel understood the girl's feelings. She'd been an

only child until a few months ago when her twin sister, Brooke, had shown up at her door. Best day of her life.

"Maybe you'll get your wish and your parents will have another baby someday." Why did she hate the thought of Kase with another woman? It had been years since he'd left here, and since he'd left her.

Addy looked at her with tears in her eyes. "We can't have any more babies…'cause my mommy died."

Oh, my God. She hadn't heard that bit of news. "Oh, sweetheart, I'm so sorry." Laurel reached for the tiny girl and pulled her into her arms. Warmth spread through her as she inhaled the soft powdery scent of a sobbing Addy. Her heart ached for the child, wishing she could help her more.

Finally the girl stopped crying, but Laurel continued to rub her back. "You are lucky you have your dad and your grandpa to take care of you."

Addy raised her head. "My daddy loves me and so does Papa." Her lips trembled again. "But my mommy didn't."

"Oh, Addy, that's not true."

The little girl brushed away tears from her cheeks and nodded. "She said I was a bad little girl. Then she went away and never came back."

Kase stood outside his daughter's bedroom, his fists clenched at his sides as he listened to the conversation. *Damn you, Johanna.* Yet his wife didn't deserve all the blame. He hadn't been around for his daughter, either. He was ashamed he'd allowed the abuse to happen. What kind of father did that make him?

Then he heard Laurel's soothing voice. "I can't imagine you were ever a bad girl, Addy. Look how nice you treat your dollies. I bet your mother was just having a bad day."

He stole another glance inside to see Laurel brush back his child's hair gently. "We all have bad days," she repeated.

Addy sat up and Laurel used the bottom of her shirt to wipe away the child's tears.

"So Mommy didn't mean it?" Addy asked.

"Of course not. She was probably tired. I'm sure she would be so proud of you for being such a good girl for your daddy."

"I am, 'cause he's so sad. I'm good for Papa Gus, too. I help him with the dishes, and I go get things 'cause his hip hurts a lot."

"What a good helper you are. And you're only four years old."

Kase's heart tripped at the sight of his daughter's sudden smile. He moved out of view but listened to the sound of their laughter. Guilt washed over him, thinking about all the selfish choices he'd made in the past ten years. And it'd all started with Laurel Quinn.

AFTER PULLING HIMSELF TOGETHER, Kase headed back downstairs. If he didn't have enough to deal with, there was now this to go with his daughter's adjustment to living here, the legal fight with his in-laws and his father's hip surgery.

Besides facing the possibility of a pregnant mare, Laurel was in this house. Pretty Laurel Quinn had been his girlfriend when they both were in high school. There had been a time when she'd spent more time here than at her house, especially that last summer before he'd gone off to college. Their relationship lasted for a little while longer until he realized that Laurel would never want the same things he did. He came home for holiday break and ended it soon after.

He shook away the memory of that day when he'd told her goodbye. Several times in the past few years, he'd questioned his decisions, but he couldn't change them. Now he was back to square one, and living in Hidden Springs again.

Since being back, he'd expected to run into Laurel occasionally, just not having her dumped on his doorstep. And not looking so fresh and pretty, and with a shapely body wrapped up in a pair of snug jeans and a Henley shirt. She'd turned his head a long time ago and nearly kept him from his dream. He couldn't let it happen again, even if they were tied together with a possible foal.

Kase walked into the small country kitchen and looked around to see the sorry shape of the room. The peeling paint on the walls was the same color as when he left, along with the worn vinyl floor and ancient appliances. If he was going to be home, he needed to do some remodeling.

His father turned from the counter, carrying two mugs of coffee. The older man made his way across the kitchen, his limp more pronounced than earlier. He probably hadn't taken any pain pills. Stubborn man.

Kase went to him. "Here, let me get those."

His father glared. "Getting out of my way is the only help I need, thank you."

Meeting his steely-gray gaze, Kase quickly moved out of the way.

At sixty-five, Gus Rawlins was tall and still slender. His face was weathered from years in the sun and his gray hair was thinning under the battered cowboy hat he wore at all times, except inside. He had a bum hip from his rodeo days long ago, then the years in the saddle, training his quarter horse.

Gus made his way to the kitchen table without spilling

a drop. He sat down and doctored his coffee with cream and sugar.

His father nodded toward him. "Aren't you going to drink yours?"

Kase took a sip, then asked, "How do you feel about what happened with Honor's Promise?"

The old man tried to hide his grin behind his mug. "I've heard good things about that stallion. If I'd been able, I'd have bought that animal myself. We might just get a good colt out of this…accident." His father raised an eyebrow. "Question is, how do you feel about Laurel being here?"

He shrugged. "We have some history, but that was years ago."

"All that money spent on your law school paid off," his father said. "You've gotten pretty good at dodging a question."

Kase refused to rise to the bait.

His father took a hearty sip. "All I know is the smile I saw on that little girl's face and it made my day. And Laurel Quinn was the cause of that."

"What about the fact you and the Quinns are dreaded enemies?"

Gus waved a hand. "Things have changed with the passing of the years. The last time Rory and I talked we couldn't seem to remember what all the hoopla was about."

Kase blinked in surprise. "It was about land boundaries, which isn't hoopla."

His father glared. "Well, it's settled now. All legal, too. Had a lawyer draw up papers and everything."

Kase tensed. "You had a lawyer? Dad, I'm your lawyer, and your son. Should I have known about this?"

Gus directed his gaze at him. "I did contact you," he

insisted. "I called your house and talked to your wife, Johanna. She said she'd let you know, but you never called me back." He shrugged. "I figured you were too busy, so we used Rory's lawyer."

Kase cursed, but the fact was he hadn't been home much. He'd been working twelve-hour days and weekends, trying to make partner. And when he was home, he fought with Johanna. "I'm sorry, Dad. I never got the message."

"It's not important now."

"The hell it isn't. Dammit, Johanna had no business in keeping your call from me."

Gus raised his hand. "I won't speak ill of the dead, and she was your wife."

If his father only knew. Kase sighed. "And she was Addy's mother, too." That had been what Gus had done over the years after Kase's mother left them. He'd never breathed a bad word about Liz Rawlins.

Gus nodded, then he abruptly changed the subject. "So what do you think of Laurel?"

He wasn't ready to talk about this. "What's to think about?"

"Maybe how pretty she is? And how she's building a pretty good reputation around here with her training horses."

Kase didn't want to think about how good she looked, or how he reacted to just seeing her again. "She was always pretty, and she's always loved horses. Remember how she used to watch you work the horses, and ask you dozens of questions?"

Gus grinned. "That she did. And looks like she got herself a good-looking stallion."

"He doesn't seem to be trainable. Look how he took off."

Gus laughed. "Now, I know you're not that old, son. That horse caught whiff of a mare in season, and nothing could stop him from getting to her."

Kase's thoughts suddenly turned to the teenage boy who had ridden off with his girl to steal some time alone. Laurel Quinn in his arms was like a dream. The taste of her mouth…

Suddenly he heard the sound of his daughter's giggles as she rushed into the kitchen. "Daddy! Daddy!" The tiny girl stopped in front of his chair. "Laurel and me had so much fun."

"I'm glad." He hugged her. But his gaze went to the woman who stood in the doorway, her long slender frame—but her subtle curves were visible to him. Even years later, he remembered her body. Those long legs, and how those firm breasts brushed against his chest. A sudden stirring began low in his gut.

His daughter's small hand nudged at him. "Daddy?"

He blinked back to the present. "What, sweetie?"

"Can Laurel spend the night with us?"

LAUREL FELT THE HEAT rush up her neck. She couldn't even look at Kase. Would he think she put his daughter up to asking? The man holding the child wasn't the same boy who'd left here years ago, and she wasn't the same person, either. The last thing she wanted was to get more involved with the man who'd already broken her heart.

She quickly made her feelings known. "Addy, I'm sorry, but I can't stay tonight."

The little girl went to her, wrapping those tiny arms around her legs. "But you're my friend, you said so."

Laurel knelt down. "I am your friend, but that doesn't mean I stay here all the time. I have to go work my horses, but I'll come back to see you. But tonight, I have a date with a very special man."

Addy's eyes lit up. "Is he a prince?"

Laurel couldn't help but smile. "I think he is. He's my dad, but I have to share him with another princess, my sister, Brooke."

"Your sister?" Kase said.

She stole a glance at the man and nodded. "A long story, but a happy one." She kissed Addy's cheek. "My daddy is taking me out to dinner with my sister."

Addy jumped up and down. "Can I go, too?"

Kase stood. "Addison Marie, it is not polite to ask to be invited."

"Maybe another time," Laurel said, wondering how she would get out of this. "I think your daddy and Papa need you here to help with supper. How about when I come back to check on the mare in a few days?"

"To see if she has a baby in her tummy?"

"That's right." Laurel fought a grin as she hugged the little girl. "So we'll say goodbye for now. You be good and I'll see you soon."

"I'll be good, I promise."

Laurel stood. "I better get back before they send out a search party."

"Glad to see you again, pretty girl," Gus said and hugged her. "Don't be a stranger, you hear?"

She forced a smile. "I won't. You take care of yourself."

She looked at Kase. "Goodbye, Kase." She started for the door.

"Daddy, you didn't hug Laurel."

Laurel tensed, seeing the stern look on Kase's face.

"You're right, Addy, I didn't."

He went to her, wrapped his arms around her and

pulled her close. At the feel of Kase's hard body against her, the years suddenly melted away. His familiar scent, which she'd know in the darkness, nearly brought tears to her eyes.

As he finally released her, he said, "I'll walk you out."

"There's no need, Kase."

He tensed. "I said I would walk you out." He opened the screen door and motioned for her to go through.

She stiffened, but she wasn't going to argue with this man, not in front of his daughter. She stepped off the porch and started toward the corral where the ATV was parked.

"Hey, slow down."

She didn't look at him. "I don't take orders from you or any man."

"Whoa, I didn't give you orders… Sorry, I guess I did, but I wanted to talk to you." His long stride easily kept up with her pace. "I wanted to thank you for what you did for Addy."

Darn it. That took the fight right out of her. "She's easy to be nice to. Sorry about your wife. That's got to be hard on both of you."

"Yeah, it's been a difficult year."

Those gray eyes met her gaze. She could see the pain. He must have loved his wife a lot. She wasn't sure she could deal with him being around again. Not that she had any remaining feelings for the man. "So being home might help you both."

"Looks like I don't have much choice in the matter."

That bothered Laurel. Seemed he hadn't changed his feelings about life here. "There's always a choice, Kase. You could just leave again."

She started to walk away, then he took hold of her arm and stopped her. His touch seared through her shirt, reminding her of years ago. Although she'd been young, she'd still never experienced the depth of desire as she had with Kase.

"I'm not leaving, Laurel, at least not for now. Dad needs surgery, and his rehab could take months. Then there's Addy, and her world has been turned upside down. She needs a stable home."

"As long as you're there for her, Addy will have all the stability she needs." She pulled out of his grip. "So, I guess we're going to be neighbors again."

He released a long breath. "Look, Laurel, it's been ten years. I would think we could be civil."

She smiled to keep from slugging the man. "I thought I was being civil." She released a breath. "Okay, I'll admit, you did hurt me. I was eighteen, but don't think that I've been mourning you all these years."

Kase glanced away, and even his profile was gorgeous. "I know, I heard about you getting married."

She was trying really hard to keep her emotions in check, but it was difficult. "Then you probably heard the rest of the story. The groom took off before the nuptials. It seems I have that effect on men." She marched off toward the vehicle, climbed in and started the engine, then shot off. She finally let the tears flow.

Chapter Three

That evening, Laurel sat at the picnic-style table of her favorite restaurant, Joe's Barbecue Smokehouse. In front of her was a huge sampler platter of ribs. Untouched. The cause of her distraction and her lack of appetite was Kase Rawlins. Seeing him today had caused a reaction she didn't need or want. Could her personal life get any more pathetic?

"Laurel, you aren't eating," her sister said.

Laurel looked across the table at her twin sister, Brooke Landry. They weren't identical, with Brooke's hair a darker blond, and her face a little longer, but close enough.

They'd met for the first time only last fall when their biological mother, suffering from Alzheimer's, told Brooke she had a twin whom she'd given to their father to raise. Seemed their father, rodeo star Rory Quinn, had been in Las Vegas for the NFR and met singer Coralee Harper. Twin daughters were the result of the brief union, but Rory knew about only one of his children, until Brooke showed up at his door. And Laurel was more than happy to have her here permanently. She got her wish when Brooke had fallen in love and married their neighbor Trent Landry, and now they were expecting a baby soon.

"Sorry, I was just thinking about what happened today with Wind."

Her father spoke in between bites of his ribs. "I told you that horse would be trouble."

Rory Quinn was a big man with green eyes the same as hers and Brooke's. He had thick gray hair and a deep, rich laugh. His face was wrinkled from the sun and years of ranching. He and her mother, Diane, had always been there for her.

"Well, he's worth it," Laurel said. "And he's going to make money."

Rory shook his head. "You're lucky you're not getting sued for what that crazy stallion did today. And now that Kase is home, and with him being a lawyer and all, he could cause you problems."

Would Kase do that?

Brooke's eyes brightened. "Yes, tell us about seeing Kase Rawlins."

Even torture wouldn't make Laurel admit that the man got her pulse revving once again. "There's nothing much to tell, really. Of course he wasn't happy about what happened to his mare. What surprised me was that he owns a horse."

Brooke picked up her short rib. "No, I mean tell me about seeing Kase again. Does he look as good as you remember?"

Laurel glanced at her father and he didn't look pleased, and she figured he'd probably remain that way no matter what answer she gave. Why would he be? His daughter's track record with men had been lousy. "It's been a long time since Kase left, but yes, he's still a good-looking man."

Her father spoke up. "Back then, you both were too

young to be so serious. I'm grateful you both went your separate ways. You both needed to concentrate on college."

That had been another sore subject between them. Her parents weren't happy when Laurel hadn't finished college. Instead, she decided to come back to breed and train quarter horses.

"You and Mom fell in love in high school. You didn't go to college." Laurel didn't want to talk about this anymore and raised her hand to stop any further comment from her father. "Let's go to a safer subject." She turned to her sister. "Has Trent painted the baby's room yet?"

Brooke beamed. "Yes, he finished the nursery yesterday. Tonight, he's putting together the crib." She took a drink of her water. "You know the one we both liked? The Child Craft? Trent liked the dark wood. He said it was more masculine for a boy."

Laurel had known their neighbor Trent Landry all her life. He'd been like a brother to her, since their parents, Wade Landry and Rory Quinn, had traveled the rodeo circuit in their younger days. After Wade's death, Trent came home and took over the Lucky Bar L Ranch. Laurel couldn't have been any happier when Trent and Brooke fell in love last fall. At least sometimes love worked out.

Suddenly Laurel heard her name, and she turned and searched the crowded room. Then she spotted the familiar little girl running toward her. "Laurel! Laurel!"

"Addy?" Laurel opened her arms just as the tiny child landed there. "What a surprise." A shock was more like it. "What are you doing here?"

Addy stood back. "I did a good job picking up my toys, so Daddy said we could go out to eat, too. He said he needed a break from cooking. Papa Gus, too." She glanced around the table and saw Brooke, then turned back to Laurel. "She looks just like you."

The group laughed. "That's because she's my twin sister," Laurel said. "We look alike, just like your dollies."

The child looked around the table. "Hi, I'm Addy and I'm four years old." She looked at Rory. "Are you Laurel's prince?"

Her father seemed to be flustered by the question. "I think I'm too old to be a prince, but she's my princess. So is my other daughter, Brooke."

Brooke waved. "Hi, Addy."

Those big blue eyes rounded as she cupped her tiny hands around her mouth and whispered loudly to Laurel. "She has a baby in her tummy."

Laurel bit back a smile. "Yes, she does."

The little girl walked around to the other side of the table, totally entranced with Brooke's expanded belly.

"I'm having a little boy," Brooke said. "We're going to name him Christopher."

"Oh, I like that name. I have a baby doll named Bobby, and I let Laurel hold him when she came in my room."

Brooke's gaze landed on Laurel's. "Really? I didn't know that."

Suddenly Laurel began to search the area for Kase. She finally saw him, helping a slower-moving Gus across the restaurant. He didn't look happy to see where his daughter had gone.

When they arrived at the table, Laurel couldn't seem to take her eyes off the man. He had on a pair of dark jeans and a blue oxford dress shirt. His sandy-blond hair was neatly combed, only making her want to mess it up. Whoa. Where did that come from?

"We seem to keep running into each other." Kase stated the obvious.

"This time it isn't my fault," she told him, knowing

everyone's eyes were on them. Darn, did the man have to look so good? "My horse is home in the barn."

Kase raised an eyebrow. "You sure about that?"

Rory was on his feet shaking Gus's hand. Then he turned to Kase. "Good to see you again, Kase." He reached out a hand.

Kase shook his hand. "It's good to see you, too."

Rory glared at his daughter. "I also heard about what happened today."

Kase nodded. "Dad assures me that it'll be fine, no matter what the outcome." His attention went across the table to Brooke. "Well, so the rumors are true, there is another one. You must be Brooke."

Brooke smiled. "Yes, I am. Nice to finally meet you, Mr. Rawlins."

"Call me Kase, please. This is my father, Gus."

Kase's father smiled. "You're a lucky man, Quinn, to have two beautiful daughters."

Rory beamed. "That I am. And you have a budding beauty in your granddaughter."

Brooke spoke up. "She is precious."

Kase's attention went to the child. "She may be, but I need to work on her running off."

"Good luck with that," Rory said. "Would you like to join us?"

"Oh, we couldn't intrude," Kase said. "We've already interrupted your supper."

"But, Daddy, I want to stay with Laurel. She's my friend."

Laurel felt tension coming from Kase. This was awkward for all of them. "Addy, I'm having a date with my prince. So why don't you have a date with your prince, your daddy?"

The little girl's eyes twinkled with excitement. "Oh, can we, Daddy?"

Kase's gaze went to Laurel. Immediately she felt heat flood through her body. Then too quickly he turned back to his daughter and said, "I would love to be with my princess." He did a slight bow and held out his hand. "Please allow me to escort you to our table, Princess Addison?"

Addy giggled, then took her father's hand and strolled off. That picture of the two caused an ache that circled her heart.

Laurel turned back to her family. Both her father and her sister were watching her. "What?"

"Seems you left out a few details about today," her father said.

"What, my stallion impregnating a neighbor's mare wasn't enough?" Laurel pretended to be interested in her food. Too bad her taste buds weren't cooperating.

"You didn't say anything about that adorable little girl being with him," Brooke said.

Laurel was confused. "Where else would she be?"

"According to Gus, she'd been living with her grandparents, the Chappells, in Denver since her mother's death. There's a big custody fight for the child."

Laurel didn't know that. Okay, she needed to get out more and talk to people instead of horses. "What? How can that be? Kase is the father and he has the right to raise his daughter."

Rory shrugged. "You would think so, but the grandparents are accusing Kase of causing his wife's death."

LATER THAT EVENING, Laurel walked around her apartment unable to sleep. The space wasn't large, but she didn't need much except a bed, a bath and a small kitchen. Not that she cooked much, but she could make sandwiches and fry eggs. That was all she had the energy for after working all day. She didn't have anyone to come home to, to hold her and love her.

She thought about Jack, and her anger began to stir. How could she have been such a fool? Maybe she hadn't loved him as she should have, but her loneliness and wanting a family of her own drove her into their arrangement.

Okay, so that wasn't the perfect scenario for marriage, but they both knew that going into it. And they did have chemistry. What she didn't expect from her husband-to-be was for him to rob her parents and Trent of their money. And for that she could never forgive him.

Now she had a bigger problem. Kase Rawlins was back in her life. She would most likely see the man when she stopped by the ranch. She wasn't going to break a promise to a little girl, especially when that child was still getting over her mother's death.

What about Kase? Was he still having trouble with his wife's passing? Of course he was. And after her father's declaration about Kase causing his wife's death, she was definitely curious to find out more.

Laurel went to the table and opened her laptop and quickly Googled Kase's name. The first reference showed he was a junior partner with the prestigious Denver law firm of Chappell, Hannett and Caruthers. It showed Kase's picture as a rising star of criminal defense. It named a famous case involving a son of an oil corporation's CEO. She moved on to his bio and his five-year marriage to Johanna Chappell Rawlins. She paused to examine the picture of the handsome Kase and his young bride, a beautiful brunette with large brown eyes.

Laurel sighed. "And to think he left a girl who wore

jeans and smelled of horses for that life." Okay, she was more the Calamity Jane type than a runway model.

She quickly did a search for Johanna Chappell Rawlins. Several pictures of the Denver socialite came up on the screen. Seemed Mrs. Rawlins, Jonnie, as her friends called her, liked to be out on the town, whether it was at parties or at fund-raisers. She was also the granddaughter of oil tycoon Henry William Cash. So Johanna Rawlins was wealthy in her own right and her family had connections. Everything Kase had been searching for when he left here ten years ago.

Laurel sank back into her chair. Kase had been right to leave her behind. She would never fit into that life, any more than Kase would fit in back here. He'd proved that when he left and never came back, not even for a visit.

She scrolled down on the computer and continued to read more. She stopped at the headline "Heiress Johanna Chappell Rawlins found dead in drug overdose. Denver Police question the husband as to his whereabouts."

She continued to read that Kase had cooperated with the police and was never charged with anything. The Chappell family felt differently.

Laurel sighed. No wonder he brought Addy back here. With the Chappells' accusation and being followed by the media, that couldn't be good for a child.

She closed her laptop. Did he really mean he was going to stay here? Could he build a new life here, or after Gus's surgery and recovery would he get bored and take off again? She couldn't afford to dream about anything happening with Kase, and definitely not act on impulse. No matter how cute his little girl was, and good-looking the man was, he was off-limits.

Her focus had to be her parents and Trent and the money she had to pay them back. There was nothing more important than that.

THE NEXT DAY, Laurel had been up early as usual. She fed the stock, exercised the horses and even got in some training. After Wind's adventure yesterday, she wanted to make sure he didn't get out again while she was in town.

Right before 9:00 a.m., she pulled her truck into the parking lot in downtown Hidden Springs, next to the professional building. She glanced up at the name Allen and Jacobs Accounting painted on the brick facade.

A few months ago, she'd applied for a part-time job to work during their busy tax season. As much as she wanted to train horses full-time, she was in debt over $30,000. That was the amount Jack had stolen from her parents and Trent when he had been their general contractor on fishing cabin projects. And if it hadn't been for her carelessness, that money might still be in the account.

She climbed out of the truck, brushed off her black pencil skirt, then reached back inside and grabbed her matching jacket off the seat. After slipping it on over her silk blouse, she headed to the door. Okay, so she enjoyed the chance to work with numbers all day, at least until tax season was over, and she was paid well.

She greeted the receptionist. "Hi, Melody."

"Good morning, Laurel."

Melody Hayes was happily married with two kids. A picture of her son, Parker, and daughter, Claire, sat on her desk like a shrine.

With a smile, Laurel continued through the double doors to the main room, where several cubbies were divided by glass partitions. She went to hers and began to sort through the new files on her desk.

Two hours later, she looked up from her computer. She raised her hands over her head and worked to stretch out the kinks from her back. That was when she heard the voices. She looked from her cubby to see Mr. Allen talking with a client outside his office. Not just any client, it was Kase. Oh, no, what was he doing here?

She moved back inside her space, hoping that he wouldn't see her, but then she heard her name called.

"Laurel!"

Suddenly Addy Rawlins stood in her doorway.

"Oh, Addy. Hi."

The little girl grinned as she strolled in and up to the desk. "What are you doing here?"

"Well, this is where I work. What are you doing here?"

"I got to come with Daddy. He said he needs help with his money now that we live with Papa Gus."

Wonderful. Would Kase somehow blame her for this, too? "Well, Mr. Allen and Mr. Jacobs are good at that."

Then she heard that familiar voice. "Addy, where are you?"

"Oh, no. Daddy's mad."

"No, he isn't. He's just worried because he doesn't know where you are." Laurel stood up and waved. "She's with me, Kase."

Kase frowned as he came around the corner to the office. Inside, he found Laurel and Addy. Great, Laurel worked here. "Addison Rawlins, what have I told you about wandering off?"

Addy looked down at the floor. "Not to leave you." She raised her head and blinked her eyes. "I'm sorry, Daddy, but I saw Laurel and I wanted to say hi."

His anger dissolved as his heart rate slowed. He knelt down. "I know you did, but I didn't know where you went."

"I won't do it again, I promise." She wrapped her arms around his neck. "Don't be mad at me, Daddy," she whispered against his ear.

His heart squeezed tightly. "Oh, sweetheart. I'm not mad at you. I was afraid that you were lost and scared."

Addy clasped her hands together. "And you were going to save me?"

He couldn't help but smile. He kissed Addy's cheek. "I'll always save you." Holding his daughter's hand, he stood up and looked at Laurel. "Seems we keep meeting."

She nodded. "I work here a few days a week."

He couldn't help but stare at the woman whom he'd never seen dressed like this. Hair pulled into a bun, wearing a blouse and skirt. He actually saw her legs. A tingle of awareness hit him low in his belly. It had been a long time since he'd seen those legs. He shook away the memory. "So you got your accounting degree?"

"I might be a few classes short, but close enough."

Cleve Allen walked up. "Mr. Rawlins," the older man began, "is everything okay?"

"Yes, my daughter just found a friend."

Allen smiled at Laurel. "Good. Would you like to go into my office and we can have our meeting?"

Kase looked down at Addy. He wasn't sure if this was a good idea. "Maybe we should reschedule. My daughter is upset and…"

"No, don't do that," Laurel jumped in. "Addy can stay with me while you two have your meeting." Laurel looked at her boss. "Is that okay with you, Mr. Allen? I'm due for my break and I could take her into the lunch room."

"That sounds like an excellent idea, Laurel. If it's okay with Mr. Rawlins?"

Kase didn't want to feel anything, but Laurel Quinn had nixed that idea. She'd stormed back into his life and he couldn't seem to stop her.

"Of course," he said and looked down at his daughter. "Addy, you be good and stay with Laurel."

Addy took hold of Laurel's hand. "I will, Daddy, 'cause she's my best friend."

Great, just another complication added to his life. With a nod, Kase turned and followed Allen down the hall.

After Kase took a seat in a barrel chair across from the man's desk, Allen walked around the desk and sat down. "First of all, thank you for trusting our firm to handle your finances, Mr. Rawlins."

Kase leaned back in his chair. "The main reason I came to you was for my father's business. He's a quarter horse trainer, but I'm not sure if he'll be able to continue his work. I want to make sure he has an income to live on." Kase had done well for himself in Denver. And although he hadn't made partner at the firm, his income was quite impressive. "I've already invested in the business with a brood mare, and I plan to do some improvements." After all, his father was just sixty-five, and he could continue to do his training if only in hiring personnel. "Also I have my daughter's trust from her deceased mother. That's handled by a bank in Denver. As of now, the trustee is her grandfather. I'm hoping to change that in the future."

Allen took notes. "We'll see if we can assist you in that trust transfer." He arched an eyebrow. "Will you be strictly working with your father, or opening your own law practice?"

"I'm not ready to make that decision." The type of law he'd practiced for Chappell had left a bad taste in his mouth. He'd sold his soul for money. Now that Johanna was gone, he had to worry about what damage her lifestyle had done to Addy. Even though the four-year-old was worth millions, she needed a lot more than money.

She needed stability and love. He'd hoped by coming back here he could do more for her. His thoughts turned to Laurel Quinn. It seemed that she was doing a much better job with his daughter than he was.

Chapter Four

Two hours later, Kase had finished with his financial meeting and ended up at the Rocky Mountain Grill for lunch. The place was a mix of fifties-style diner with a Western twist. The storefront restaurant hadn't changed since he used to hang out here in high school.

He glanced across the table at Laurel, and a funny feeling rushed over him. Suddenly he thought about the cocky-as-hell seventeen-year-old boy who'd dated the pretty freshman with the big green eyes. She'd been into horses, but he'd quickly changed her interest to him. He also remembered how he used to sit in this same booth and share some fries…and a few kisses.

Then came the day he'd broken her heart and went off to what he thought would be a better life. The joke was on him. It seemed everything he'd been looking for wasn't found in Denver. The big home, beautiful wife and illustrious career had gone down the tubes. The only thing that mattered now was Addy. He tensed. He would do anything to keep her safe and with him.

At the sound of Addy's soft sigh, he looked down to find that she was snuggled up beside Laurel, fast asleep.

He started to stand. "Let me take her."

Laurel waved him off. "She's fine."

"I should move her so you can at least eat your lunch. You have to be uncomfortable."

"It's okay." She continued to rub Addy's arm. "Let her sleep. I have a feeling she's missing her naptime."

He raised an eyebrow. "Don't you know naps are for babies?"

That got a smile from Laurel, and his pulse sped up.

"Then I guess I'm still a baby because I like naps," she confessed. "But then I'm up at five."

He glanced again at his daughter and how Laurel's hand stroked her lovingly. He couldn't remember his wife ever spending much time with their child. Addy was probably starved for some affection. Guilt hit him deep in his chest. He should have been there for his child, too.

Laurel got his attention when she said, "I bet she was up this morning at five."

"Yeah, you know my dad. He needed to feed the horses."

"Where is Gus?"

"I dropped him off to visit his friend Charlie Cleveland." He checked his watch. "But I'll need to pick him up soon and take him to his appointment at the clinic."

The waitress arrived at their table and set down their plates. "Would you like anything else?" the girl asked.

He glanced at Laurel and she shook her head. "We're fine, thank you."

Laurel took a bite of a french fry. "Oh, so good." She moaned in pleasure. "I don't get much of a chance to indulge in Rocky's hamburgers and fries."

Kase tried to concentrate on his food but found he'd rather watch Laurel.

When she frowned at him, he realized he'd been staring again and picked up his hamburger. He took a big bite. "So good. I haven't had a good burger in a long time."

Laurel waved another fry before popping it into her mouth. "So the big-time lawyer can't be caught eating a double-stack burger with everything, including onions?"

"Most of my clients prefer something more than a hamburger lunch, especially for what it costs them to keep us on retainer."

Laurel knew it wasn't a good idea to accept Kase's lunch invitation, but here she was sitting across from him. Even though it had been Addy who'd invited her, Kase had tossed in he wanted to thank her for watching his daughter during his meeting.

She was so out of her league. This wasn't the Kase Rawlins who'd left here ten years ago. She didn't know how to play the game. She'd proved that with her lousy record with men. "You must be good at what you do if you've made junior partner so soon." She took a big bite of her sandwich.

His gaze shot to hers, his gray depths suddenly dark and searching. "So you checked me out."

When would she learn to keep her mouth shut? She shrugged, trying to act like it didn't matter much. "It's easy to Google a person." She took another french fry. "Seems you got everything you wanted after you left here."

He paused, then said, "Sometimes we get confused about what we want, especially when we're so young."

Her heart stopped, then sped up again. "You didn't want to be a great criminal defense attorney?"

"Great is a stretch," he said. "I had one landmark case. I got lucky with some evidence and with a good cyber investigator, so I was able to prove my client's innocence."

Laurel couldn't help but get caught up in his enthusiasm as he talked about his case. No doubt he was born to be a lawyer. Hadn't he told her that was his passion from day one of their dating?

Now he was back in Hidden Springs, widowed, with a young daughter. Would he be changing careers and staying permanently? "I think you're being modest."

Kase leaned back in his seat. He didn't want to talk about himself or the future, since he wasn't sure about anything but keeping Addy. His attention went to Laurel as she lovingly brushed his daughter's hair back. Her gaze met his. Those green eyes had always been able to turn him inside out.

Laurel sighed. "Addy's had a lot to deal with in her short life, especially losing her mother so young, and moving back here. All those changes can't be easy for her."

"I guess so." He didn't want to hash over Johanna's lack of mothering. "But I want to concentrate on building a new life for us here."

She arched an eyebrow. "So you're staying? Permanently?"

A funny feeling came over him as he looked across the table at the beautiful woman and wondered why he ever left. He nodded slowly.

She smiled and his breath locked in his chest.

"Isn't it funny how life works out?" she questioned. "I mean, the last place you wanted to be was in Hidden Springs."

"There isn't much opportunity in a small town for defense attorneys." He paused. "Look, Laurel, I know I didn't exactly treat you fairly when we broke up. I was young and selfish…"

She sweetly replied, "And I was a rancher's daughter who didn't fit into your plan to make a life in the big city."

He glanced away, wishing she'd hit him with anger,

instead of being nice. He could fight her fury, remembering how the teenage Laurel would stand her ground against him. "What did I know back then?"

"A lot. You followed your dream, Kase. You made a name for yourself with your perseverance and drive. You need to be proud of that."

And his family suffered. "It doesn't seem that important now."

Silence hung between them in the noisy diner that was filling with other customers. "So what are you going to do?" Laurel finally asked. "Retire? Help Gus with breeding and training horses?"

He frowned. "I'm Dad's partner, but he's the expert and has the reputation. With my financial backing, I hope we can rebuild the business. Dad's had some rough times lately. And with Honor's Promise's possible pregnancy, looks like I just launched my new career."

Laurel huffed out a breath. "Again, I'm so sorry about what happened yesterday with Wind."

He reached across the table and touched her hand. He ignored the warm sensation and said, "I was teasing."

Laurel smacked his arm playfully, needing to lose his connection. His touch did more than she was willing to admit. "You won't be laughing when you see the beautiful foal you'll be getting for free."

He opened his mouth to speak, but his phone rang. "It's Gus." He put it against his ear. "Hey, Dad. Are you ready?" He listened a moment. "Okay, I'll be by as soon as I get Addy moving." Ending the call, he looked down at his little girl. Laurel didn't miss the emotion in his eyes.

He slid out of the booth, leaned over the sleeping child and shook her gently. "Hey, baby, it's time to wake up."

Addy's eyelids fluttered and her tiny hands came up to rub them.

"Daddy?"

"Hi, sweetie. We need to go get Papa and take him to the doctor."

The child sat up and looked at Laurel, then burst into tears. "But I didn't get to eat lunch with Laurel."

At Kase's panicked look, Laurel stepped in. "It's okay, sweetie. You can still eat with me." She knew she was overstepping her bounds. "And your dad can take Papa Gus to the doctor and you and I can finish our lunch."

Kase frowned. "Laurel, I can't expect you to keep watching Addy." He checked the clock on the wall. "Besides, don't you have to go back to work?"

"I only work three mornings during tax season. The afternoons, I work at my main business, Quinn Stables and Training."

The child's tears stopped immediately and Laurel looked back at Kase, daring him to say differently. "And when we're finished eating, I'll take Addy home with me. I have a new client coming by with her horse today. Since the Bucking Q is on your way home, you can pick her up there."

"That's too much to ask of you."

"I know that," she told him, "but you need to get Gus to the doctor, and I bet he's being stubborn about going. So don't lose this opportunity to get him help for his hip."

Kase smiled at her, and she felt her guard slipping, darn it. "Thank you. I owe you big-time."

"You sure do, and I plan to collect."

"Gladly," he told her. His gray eyes flashed heat, then he looked back to his daughter. "Do what Laurel tells you, and I'll pick you up in a few hours." With Addy's nod, he exchanged cell phone numbers with Laurel and stood, then pulled out his keys. "Since you'll need her car seat, we should just exchange cars. Where are you parked?"

"Next to the office. It's the black truck with the Bucking Q Ranch logo on the side." She reached into her purse and handed over her keys.

He grabbed them as he leaned down to kiss his daughter's forehead, and she caught a whiff of his aftershave. The subtle fragrance got her motor running. He raised his head and his gaze locked on hers. "Thank you again."

"Daddy, don't forget to kiss Laurel, too."

He winked. "I wouldn't forget that."

Her heart began to pound as his head descended toward hers and he brushed a soft kiss against her cheek. He picked up the check from the table. "Goodbye, Laurel."

"Goodbye," she answered, but her voice didn't sound like hers.

Unable to help herself, she watched as the good-looking man dressed in a pair of dark jeans and boots walked to the cashier and paid the bill. Then he started out and held the door for a woman, then nodded a greeting and walked out.

She had to stop this, realizing her heart was still racing. Kase was not the man for her. Not ten years ago, and definitely not now.

She felt a tug on her arm and looked down at Addy. "Do I have to eat my fruit?" she asked.

This child could steal her heart if she let her. "Maybe two bites and eat some of your hamburger. Then we'll go see my horses."

She was rewarded with a big smile, and the girl picked up her fork and began to eat. Laurel wished she could stimulate her appetite, but Kase had her stomach in knots. She didn't even want to think about what he could do to her heart again.

"DAD, YOU NEED to listen to the doctor. He's telling you that you need this surgery. It's the only thing that will get rid of the pain and help you walk easier again."

Gus Rawlins sat in the chair in the medical office and glanced between his son and the young doctor who didn't look much older. "Will I be able to ride again?"

The fortysomething orthopedist adjusted his wire-rim glasses. "After a successful surgery, many patients go back to normal activities. I'm not sure if it's wise for you to spend all day in a saddle, but I've seen people do it." He smiled. "The important key is getting a good rehab program."

Gus didn't look convinced. "And what if it makes my hip worse?"

Dr. Copeland folded his arms. "I perform this type of surgery every week, Mr. Rawlins, and I haven't had many complications. That is, unless the patient doesn't work at rehab."

Gus looked at his son. "That's another thing. I don't need to go into any nursing home. What if I don't ever get out?"

Kase's heart sank. Did his father really think that? Guilt washed over him. He wasn't going to abandon him again. "They can't keep you, Dad. If they try, you can have your lawyer sue them." Kase smiled, trying to make light of the situation.

Gus looked at the doctor. "He's got a smart mouth because he's a lawyer." He sighed. "Okay, I'll do the surgery, but I want to do the rehab at the house."

"Dad…"

Gus raised his hand. "I need to make sure my horses are looked after. And what about Addy? Who will watch after her? I don't want to worry her because I'm not there. She's already lost people…"

Kase wasn't sure how to handle this. He looked at the doctor for help.

"I have a list of excellent physical therapists who

could come out to the house," the doctor said. "It could be expensive, though. Your insurance may not cover all the expense."

"If this helps my father, I'll pay extra for a therapist to come to the ranch." He frowned at his father. "So when can you schedule the surgery?"

The doctor looked over his computer screen. "I have next Friday at seven in the morning."

They both looked at Gus. Finally his father relented. "Okay, I'll do it, but not for you—it's for my granddaughter. I made a lot of promises to her, and I plan to be around to make good on all of them."

Kase wanted to know what his father was up to, but right now he'd settle for what he could get from the man.

THREE HOURS LATER, Laurel watched as her new client drove away pulling an empty trailer. Left behind was a beautiful three-year-old roan mare named Ruby Ridge. Laurel was going to be training the quarter horse for reining competitions.

She was excited about working her horses through the precise patterns of circles, spins and stops. The new corral her father built was a perfect area for the Western-style dressage.

The past few months she'd been working one of Trent's horses, Red Baron, a beautiful stallion showing plenty of promise. Now she had Ruby Ridge and a chance to prove herself. With the owner, Kat Bryce, willing to help her horse learn, and Laurel putting in the practice time, how could she pass it up? She'd be building a reputation, too, and the money she'd make would go into the fund to pay back her parents.

Hearing her name, Laurel turned to see her mother and little Addy walking down from the house.

She smiled and waved back at her mom, a woman who was an attractive brunette in her early fifties. The best mother ever, even after she'd discovered last fall that Diane Quinn wasn't her biological mother.

That discovery came out when Brooke Harper arrived at the ranch, claiming to be her twin sister. And her biological mother was really a Las Vegas singer, Coralee Harper, who spent a weekend with their father, Rory Quinn, before her parents got married.

All these years, Rory knew about only one child, Laurel. When Coralee was diagnosed with early onset Alzheimer's, she wanted to see her other daughter before losing all memory and sent Brooke to find her. Now, seven months later, Coralee had been moved into a nursing home only a few miles from the ranch.

Brooke, who'd been raised by the woman, visited her almost daily, and Laurel got there once or twice a week. Some days Coralee knew her, and some days not. Coralee might be her biological mother, but nothing could ever change Laurel's feelings for the woman who'd raised her.

"Hey, Mom. Hey, Addy."

Addy smiled. "Hi, Laurel. Your mommy showed me your old bedroom. I saw your special dollies."

Laurel grinned. "You mean Amy and Betsy?"

The child nodded her head, causing her curls to bounce. "Mimi said she wants to keep them for when you have a little girl, so she can play with them."

Laurel looked at her mother and mouthed, "Mimi?"

Diane shrugged. "I didn't know what she should call me." She smiled. "She's so adorable."

Oh, no. She didn't want her mother to hatch a scheme to get her and Kase back together. As far as she was concerned she'd sworn off men. She leaned forward and whispered, "Be careful. This little conniver will steal your heart."

"I think she already has," her mother admitted.

Just then she saw her truck coming up the road. It parked next to the barn, the door opened and Kase stepped out. Her breath caught when he straightened to his full six-foot-one frame, exposing the width of his broad shoulders and his narrow waist. His long, easy strides took him around to the passenger side, where he helped Gus climb out.

"Daddy! Papa!" Addy cried and took off running toward them.

Kase turned in time to catch the enthusiastic child in his arms, then swung her around in the air. Addy giggled in delight.

"Will you look at that?" her mother said with a sigh. "There's just something about a man holding a child that's so appealing."

Laurel couldn't stop staring when Kase hoisted his daughter high into his arms and kissed her cheek, then held her while Gus kissed her, too. She felt her own chest tighten on seeing the loving scene.

Kase looked toward her and waved. As his father moved slowly with his cane, the threesome made their way up the drive. Laurel and her mother met them halfway.

"Hello, Laurel," Kase greeted.

Her heart raced. "Hi, Kase. Gus."

Gus nodded and looked at her mother. "It's nice to see you again, Diane."

"Good to see you, too, Gus. It's been too long."

Kase turned to her mother. "How are you, Mrs. Quinn?"

Laurel watched as her mother blushed. "Oh, please, Kase, call me Diane."

He nodded, but Addy said, "I get to call her Mimi, Daddy."

The blush deepened. "I wasn't sure what to have her call me."

"That's okay, as long as she's respectful."

"She's been nothing but polite, and a sweetheart."

"Did she talk you to death?"

Diane smiled brightly. "I'm used to it." She hugged her daughter. "I raised this little chatterbox."

Laughter rang out in the group.

Addy touched her dad's face and made him turn toward her. "We made peanut butter cookies. I got to make the crisscross marks on top."

"Wow, it sounds like you had fun today."

Diane looked at Gus, leaning on his cane. "Gus, please come up to the porch and sit down."

"We should go," Kase said. "I've already taken advantage of your and Laurel's time."

"Nonsense," Diane said. "In fact, I'd like to extend an invitation for supper."

Laurel froze. What was her mother doing?

Kase spoke up first. "Oh, Mrs.... Diane, we can't intrude."

"You're not intruding at all. It's just a big pot of beef stew and some homemade bread."

Gus groaned. "And peanut butter cookies for dessert?"

Addy nodded. "Daddy, I want to stay. I didn't get to play with Laurel. She had to work all day."

Laurel caught the mischief in Kase's eyes before he turned to his daughter. "Maybe Laurel's too tired to play."

All eyes turned to her. What was she to do? As much as she didn't need to get involved in Kase's life, she couldn't seem to help herself. "Maybe we can play for a little bit before supper."

"Yeah." Little Addy grinned at getting her way. She squirmed out of her daddy's arms and walked ahead with Laurel's mother and Gus.

He reached out and touched Laurel's forearm. "I truly didn't mean to tie up your entire day."

She looked at his incredible eyes. Her breath locked in her lungs and she glanced away to gather herself. "Not a problem."

She started toward the house. "Come on, they'll wonder where we are."

No matter how much fun she had with Addy today, it was not good to get any more involved with a man who'd already broken her heart once. But here she was back in line to let it happen again.

Chapter Five

After two heaping bowls of Diane Quinn's beef stew, Kase had been easily convinced to go out to have a look at one of Laurel's mares. Even suspicious that his dad was playing matchmaker, he followed Laurel out the door, leaving Addy happily occupied by Diane, Rory and Gus.

Kase stepped inside the immaculate barn with only a faint scent of horses and hay. Impressive. He looked around to see several enclosed stalls and the tack hung neatly on the wall. With Laurel's arrival, he heard several equine whinnies.

He followed her as she greeted her horses. Suddenly she stopped and he ran into her. Trying to keep his balance, he quickly grabbed her waist. But the close connection made him very aware of those once-familiar curves.

"Whoa there." Feeling the softness under his hands, it was impossible not to react, or to let her go. It had been a long time since he'd had any interest in a woman. Johanna had made sure of that.

Laurel quickly pulled away. "Sorry." She didn't look at him, just walked to one of the stalls, where the horse came to greet her. The rogue stallion's bobbing of his large head and familiar wild mane made Kase quickly recognize him.

"You already know Wind," she said.

He nodded, making eye contact with Laurel, and another zing hit him. "I have a feeling I'll be seeing those markings on his foal in about eleven months."

Laurel smiled as she rubbed the horse's nose. "Would that be so bad?"

He realized her smile had him thinking about something other than horses. "According to my dad, no. And since Gus is the expert, I'll let him handle Honor's condition."

"Isn't she your horse?"

Kase leaned against the post and nodded. "Gus was the one who suggested I buy Honor. He said she was a good investment, so I went along with him. You and I both know that Dad runs the operation. I'm still learning and adding some backing to jump-start Rawlins Horse Ranch."

"What about when Gus has his surgery? Who's going to run things then?"

"Well, there won't be much training unless I hire someone, but Dad doesn't want anyone else messing with his horses. That's why he's been so stubborn about having surgery. He refuses to be away from the ranch for any length of time."

"Then why can't you take over? As I remember, you were pretty good at working his stock."

He frowned. "I only did what Dad told me, but he did all the intricate training. Besides, who's going to be caring for Addy while I'm spending time with the horses?" He shook his head. "No, I've missed too many years with her. I refuse to hire a babysitter to be her parent. She's had too much of that already." He started off down the aisle.

Laurel stood there in shock. *He's missed too many years with her.* What did that mean? She wanted to ask him more questions, but it wasn't her business.

She caught up with him as he reached the next stall. The chestnut horse with a white star on her forehead appeared at the gate and she watched as Kase stroked her forehead. The pregnant mare ate up the attention.

Laurel immediately went to her, letting the horse nuzzle her chest. "This is Starr Gazer, my championship cutting horse. I recently bred her with Wind. She should have her foal in about six months." Laurel wrapped her arms around the horse's neck and hugged her close. "Going to be a mama soon, huh, girl?"

"I can see why Dad wanted me to see her. She's a beauty." Kase rubbed the animal's head. "What are your plans for the foal?"

"I'd love to keep her, but I'll need to sell."

She didn't miss his questioning look. "Why not hang on to the foal and train it?"

"Because I can't afford the time." She hated that she'd gotten in this position. "I have loans to pay back."

"That's rough." His gaze met hers and immediately her body shuddered, reacting to this gorgeous man. "I'm sure your dad doesn't expect you to pay him back."

Laurel glanced away, embarrassed that she'd been so gullible over Jack. "So you've heard the gossip in town about my runaway groom."

He shook his head. "Dad told me. I wondered why you never married."

She was surprised by his answer. "It seems I'm better off with horses than men."

His mouth twitched in amusement. "If that's how you feel, then you've been with the wrong men."

Her gaze shot to his, her throat suddenly dry. A flash of memories of a younger Kase appeared in her mind. That cocky grin, his tempting mouth and his tender touch… She swiftly shook them away. "Seems I have a habit of choosing wrong. You'd think after all these years, I'd learn my lesson."

Kase saw the hurt on her face, knowing she'd included him in that group. He'd give anything to take away her pain. He wanted to reach out and touch her, remembering how soft and giving she'd always been with him. He ached to find out if her mouth still tasted as sweet...

He pushed aside the image. Now wasn't the time to rehash the past.

"Look, Laurel, I know we've been thrown together these past few days, but if you want me to stay away, I'll do it." He held his breath, hoping that she wouldn't send him packing. The last thing he needed was to include her in his crazy life.

She placed her hands on her hips. "Now you tell me. Now, after I finally get a new best friend to share my dolls with. And then there's Gus. Who can give me his expertise on training? And you want to take that away."

He smiled at her joking, then he grew serious, realizing that his daughter was getting very attached to Laurel. Besides being beautiful and sexy, he'd seen how loving and caring she'd been with Addy.

"Look, Laurel, my life is unsettled to say the least. I have a daughter to raise, and a father facing surgery." He sighed. That was only the tip of his problems. "As you'll soon learn, my in-laws are suing for custody of Addy. So everything I do is under a microscope."

He saw the compassion in her eyes. "Is that because they believe you're the cause of their daughter's death?"

"Where did you hear that?"

"A newspaper article on the web."

"We'd already separated before her overdose." His gaze met Laurel's interested look. "I tried to help her, but she wouldn't go into rehab. Not even for Addy. I even went to my father-in-law, but he refused to help have his daughter committed. Bad for business, he said. So I resigned from the firm and filed for divorce."

"Was Addy living with her mother then?"

He nodded. "I'll regret that until my dying day. The only consolation was her nanny, Mary Beth, who'd been with Addy since birth and had gone with her when they'd moved into the cottage on Johanna's parents' property. At least Addy and Johanna had supervision." He stole a look at Laurel. She had every right to judge his parenting skills.

"Two weeks later, I got the call about Johanna's drug overdose."

He felt her hand on his arm. "I'm sorry, Kase."

He shrugged, ashamed that he couldn't give his wife what she needed. And questioning himself if he even tried enough to make the marriage work. "So am I."

"So you came back here?"

"Since Addy had already been staying at her grandparents', I had a tough time getting physical custody. Ben and Judith refused to give her up, but I finally got a lawyer to help me and removed her from her grandparents' home."

"They were probably upset about their daughter's death," Laurel said. "And Addy is their last connection to her."

Kase knew that wasn't true. They hadn't been that attentive with their own daughter, let alone with their granddaughter.

"Whatever the reason, they're suing me for custody." He looked at her. "I won't lose Addy, Laurel. I've done a lot of things wrong, but my daughter is the best thing in my life. I have a second chance to be a father, and I'm trying my best not to mess it up."

Laurel smiled. "You've got one thing going for you."

"What's that?"

"She adores you. You're her hero, her knight in shining armor and prince all rolled into one."

He felt his chest swell. "No, I'm just the man who prays he doesn't let her down again."

NIGHT HAD FALLEN by the time they finished the tour of the barn and started back to the house. Security lights illuminated the way as Kase found he didn't want this time with Laurel to end. It had been so long since he took time for the simpler things, such as enjoying the company of a woman.

During the years he'd been trying to make partner, he'd spent long hours working. At the time, he'd thought that was the road to success. He hadn't stopped to enjoy what he had. Right now all he could think about was what he left back in Hidden Springs.

He glanced at Laurel as she walked ahead of him. Her long legs encased in slim jeans ate up the distance to the house. He wished the trip took longer as his attention went to the gentle sway of her hips. Awareness surged through him, settling in the pit of his stomach.

They might have been just fumbling kids when he'd left for college, but that didn't mean they hadn't burned for each other. He could still feel the heat and found it difficult to keep his hands off her.

Yet the last thing he needed was another complication. His renewed attraction to Laurel could be trouble. No matter how strong that pull was, any personal relationships would be impossible now. Not until he was sure Addy's custody issue had been resolved completely.

Suddenly Laurel's voice broke through the silence. "If

you want, I can talk to Gus about trainers," she suggested. "At least give him some names that I've worked with."

Good, let's talk about a safe subject. Kase wasn't sure his dad trusted many people. "Thank you. I might have to take you up on that. With his procedure scheduled for this coming Friday, I'm running out of time."

She glanced at him. "How long does the doctor say he'll be out of commission?"

"About five days in the hospital. It's the rehab that he's balking about. He's refusing to go into a rehab facility, but it's the fastest and easiest way to get him back on his feet."

They reached the porch and Laurel said, "I think he's worried, Kase. He loves having you back home, but he doesn't want to be a burden, either."

"Well, he's being a pain in the as…bottom."

She tossed her head back and laughed. "That's quite a mouth you got, Mr. Attorney."

He smiled, too. "It's Addy's influence. She doesn't like me to say bad words."

She pushed open the back door, walked through the mudroom and into the kitchen to find the foursome at the table working on a puzzle.

Addy raised her head. "Look, Daddy, I'm helping Mimi, Pops and Papa Gus do a puzzle. It's a picture of a horse."

"And you're doing a great job." The cozy family scene gave him hope that he made the right decision to bring his daughter home.

LAUGHTER FILLED THE Quinns' kitchen as Addy entertained everyone with her silly chatter. They ate ice cream and tried to come up with more puzzle pieces.

"This is fun," she announced. "Daddy, can we get some puzzles at our house?"

"That's a great idea. When Papa Gus has to stay inside after his surgery, you can help him do puzzles."

His daughter nodded, bouncing her wayward curls against her shoulders. "I can do that." Looking around the table, she announced, "Papa Gus has a broken hip. The doctor's gonna fix it on Friday."

Suddenly Diane Quinn looked at Kase's father across the table. "Gus Rawlins, you've sat here all evening and didn't say a word to us." She folded her arms across her breasts. "What time on Friday?"

Gus glanced away, then back at her. "Seven a.m. at Mountain View Hospital."

"So I expect you have to be there much earlier. How can we help?"

Gus seemed to be at a loss. "Not sure there's much you can do."

Rory Quinn stepped in. "I can send two hands over to your place to take care of your stock. You just write down the feed mix and what needs to be done."

Kase started to answer, but his father took over. "Kase and I would appreciate that. Thank you, Rory. You're a good neighbor."

Rory gave a curt nod. "Don't mention it. I know you'd do the same for me."

Suddenly Addy looked worried. "What about me? Daddy, you said I can't go to the hospital 'cause I'm too little."

"I completely forgot about a sitter." He looked at Laurel. "Could you recommend someone?"

"Yeah, how about if she stays with me?" she said.

Addy's blue eyes sparkled. "Yeah, Daddy, that's a good idea. I can stay with Laurel."

Everyone around the table seemed to be fighting a smile. He realized his daughter had set him up. "But Laurel has her horses to train."

The child thought a minute, then said, "Maybe I can stay with Mimi and bake cookies." She turned to Diane and gave her a sweet smile. "Can we bake cookies again?"

Kase was embarrassed. "Addy, what did I say about asking?"

"I said *maybe*," Addy clarified.

The room broke into laughter. "She's got you there, son," Rory said.

"There's no *maybe* about it," Diane told her. "Addy, you are welcome here anytime. Friday is a perfect day because I planned to be inside and baking all day. In fact, Brooke is coming by."

Addy turned back to her father. "Please, Daddy? I'll be good for Mimi. And I won't be sad thinking about Papa in the hospital."

Kase realized he wouldn't have to worry about his daughter's care. "Diane and Laurel, thank you. I'd appreciate it if you would watch Addy."

His daughter cheered.

Laurel stepped in and suggested, "You should bring her by Thursday night."

"A sleepover? I never had a sleepover." Addy looked at Laurel. "Can I bring my baby dolls, too?"

Laurel went to the child and hugged her. "Of course. I'd love to play with you. We can sleep in my old bedroom upstairs."

Laurel's gaze met his. He never stood much of a chance saying no to his daughter, and with this beautiful twosome it was impossible.

AN HOUR LATER, they'd cleaned up the kitchen and convinced Addy to finish the puzzle when she came for
the sleepover. It was well past the girl's bedtime. Laurel
watched as Kase held the sleepy child in his arms. Her
heart squeezed at the tender scene. Kase made eye contact with her, then quickly glanced away and headed out
the back door.

She was a goner, and sinking further by the second.
The more time she spent with this child, she began to
think about things she didn't need to think about. Such
as starting something with Kase.

Laurel followed the group out the back door. Her
mother walked with her. "Isn't she just precious?"

"Yes, she is," Laurel agreed. "You were so good with
her today."

"I loved every minute of it." Her mother smiled
brightly. "Besides, it's good practice for when Brooke
has her baby."

Laurel hated that she envied her sister so much.
Brooke had everything she ached for—a loving husband
and child on the way. She walked outside past Gus and
her father saying their goodbyes and to the truck where
Kase was fastening Addy into her safety seat.

Once finished, he turned to her. "I can't thank you
enough for watching her today."

"Not a problem, Kase. I enjoy spending time with
Addy." *Maybe too much*, she thought.

"Still, it's not easy to take on a four-year-old. Believe
me, I know. It's a learning experience every day."

"We'll learn together." Her face flamed with em-
barrassment. "I mean, I need to learn anyway because
Brooke's having a baby."

Kase grinned, loving her openness. "I know."

When his cell phone rang, he pulled it from his pocket.

Seeing the name on the caller ID, he froze. It was his father-in-law, Ben Chappell.

"Answer it," Laurel said. "I'll stay with Addy."

He stepped away from the vehicle and out of earshot. "Rawlins here."

"Kase, it's Ben."

"What do you want, Ben?"

"You already know the answer, Kase. You need to bring my granddaughter back to Denver. She belongs here. Johanna would want her to be with us."

"You have no idea what Johanna would want." He turned to see his dad still talking with Rory and not paying any attention to him. "Or you would have tried to get her some help. So don't throw your guilt on me."

"You weren't much better," Ben tossed back. "But exposing Johanna's problems now isn't going to help, either."

"Then why, Ben? Why take me to court for Addy?" he challenged. "Johanna's secret lifestyle is all going to come out in court."

He heard Ben's stressed breathing. "And you could lose everything."

"What am I going to lose? Addy is the only thing that's important to me."

"You knew about your wife's drug abuse, too."

"The hell I did. As soon as I learned about it, I resigned from the firm and came home to take care of Addy."

"I bet I can come up with proof that you knew about the drugs and turned a blind eye."

"Hell, we'd separated by then. She'd moved home."

There was a long pause, then Ben said, "Judith and I both feel Addy will be better off with a two-parent family. We'll see you in court."

Kase cursed as he paced the driveway. His worst nightmare was coming true. He clenched his fists. He couldn't lose Addy. She was his life.

He quickly punched in his lawyer's private number. The phone rang, and Sam Gerrard, his college friend, answered, "Hey, Kase. I take it, since it's after office hours, there's a problem."

"There is. I just got a call from my father-in-law. Seems Ben's pulling out the big guns."

Kase told him about the phone call and his threats. "Is there the slightest chance they can take Addy from me?"

There was a pause, and Sam finally said, "I'm going to say if there is, it's a slim one. But Ben Chappell has a lot of influence in this area. He knows people, important people. Both Judith and Ben are well respected in the community. Judith has always been involved with charity work."

Kase turned and saw Gus heading to the truck with Rory. "And that's a reason I could lose custody of my daughter?"

"No, but with the right judge, he could see that an affluent couple raising Addy might be better than a single dad with no real income…"

Kase raked his hand through his hair in frustration. "Are you saying I need to get married to keep my daughter?"

"Not exactly, but hell, Kase, it wouldn't hurt."

"This can't be happening," he murmured. "Look, I need to get Addy home and in bed. I'll talk to you later."

He slipped his phone back into his pocket as Laurel came toward him. "Is everything okay?"

He shook his head. "That was my lawyer. Seems being a single dad isn't in my favor for my custody suit."

She cocked her head. "Really? If you were married, your chances would be better to keep Addy?"

He shrugged. "I guess. Why, are you offering?"

Chapter Six

"She's so adorable," Brooke whispered from the bedroom doorway.

Friday morning, Laurel watched a sleeping Addy curled up on the childhood bed with her baby dolls. Being the child's first sleepover, her excitement had kept everyone awake late last night. By ten o'clock this morning, Addy needed a nap and Laurel needed a break.

Careful not to disturb the child, Laurel stood and headed out the door. Her pregnant sister followed her downstairs and into the large paneled family room.

"I'm exhausted." Laurel sank into her dad's favorite chair. "I can't keep up with all that child's energy."

Brooke slowly sank down on the camel-colored sofa, then worked to get comfortable with her oversize stomach. "You wouldn't be so tired if the child didn't cling to you every minute."

Laurel studied her sister. They looked alike, with their eye and hair color, but they weren't identical. And now her sister was twenty pounds heavier with baby.

"It's because she only lost her mother less than a year ago. Besides, she didn't bother me."

"That's sad about her mother." Brooke's gaze met hers. "You know, you're quickly becoming her replacement."

"I'm her friend," Laurel clarified, realizing she was getting attached to the child, too.

"Then you better set boundaries because that little girl is looking for a mommy."

Laurel sighed. "I think she just wants a family."

"Don't we all," Brooke said.

Laurel hated that her newfound sister had such a rough upbringing in Las Vegas but was happy Brooke came here in search of her father and her twin. She also found the love of her life, Trent Landry.

Brooke's voice brought her back to reality. "And Addy's daddy is pretty handsome, too."

"Wait, aren't you married to a handsome, sexy rancher?"

"Yes, and Trent knows I'll love him to the end of time."

Suddenly Brooke's husband-in-question walked into the room. "Did I hear my name?" A big grin appeared across his handsome face as he looked at his wife.

Ex-army, Trent had warm brown eyes and still wore his dark hair short. When he folded his massive arms across his chest, he intimidated a lot of people. Laurel had known him most of her life, and he was like a big brother to her. She couldn't be happier that the two found each other.

Brooke smiled at him. "I was just telling Laurel that I only have eyes for you."

He walked across the room and dropped a heated kiss on his wife's mouth. The love these two shared for each other was obvious. She couldn't help but be a little envious of her twin, if it wasn't for the fact Brooke had never had love until she came here.

"Will you be okay if I go into town and look at some outfitter equipment? We have that fishing party coming in a few weeks."

Laurel was happy the new rental cabins her father and

Trent had partnered in were doing well. Their occupancy had been high since they opened last fall. That helped with some of the sting of Jack's betrayal.

Brooke nodded. "I'll be fine here with Diane and Laurel. Then we're going to see Coralee when Addy wakes up from her nap."

"Enjoy your day." Trent kissed her again, stroked her belly before he gave Laurel a loving pat on the head, then he left.

Brooke's eyes had a dreamy look.

Laurel laughed. "Yeah, like you'd look at another man."

Brooke brought her attention back to her sister. "I can still see that Kase Rawlins is a good-looking guy."

"Yes, he is. And I was crazy about him in high school, but he left me and became a successful lawyer at a prestigious law firm, then he married the boss's beautiful daughter. The perfect life. He didn't give a second thought to the horse-loving tomboy back home."

Brooke raised a hand. "Wait a minute." She hated seeing the pain in her sister's eyes. She doubted that Kase Rawlins thought of Laurel as a tomboy. "You're beautiful, Laurel."

Laurel glanced down at herself. "Yeah, right. I wear dusty jeans and scuffed boots." She raised her foot. "I rarely take time to wear makeup." She tugged on her braid. "And this wild hair is…"

No matter if she denied it, Brooke knew that Laurel cared about Kase. And the one time she'd met the man, she wasn't surprised that he couldn't take his eyes off her sister. "Then you need to make time for yourself. Don't hate me, but not everything is about horses."

Laurel's head swung around to her. "I have to put any extra money back into my business."

"It doesn't take much money. I could trim your hair and show you how to condition it. And as for makeup, we're Coralee's daughters. I can show you some subtle tips."

Laurel looked shocked at her suggestion. "I don't want to look like a Las Vegas lounge singer."

Brooke had been raised by a woman who spent her entire adult life trying to make her big break as a singer. Even after her mother gave away one of her daughters, Laurel, Brooke suffered from Coralee's selfishness and neglect until she came to Colorado and met her family… and Trent.

"I'm not planning on stage makeup, just some highlights for your eyes, and maybe take your hair out of that braid. Men have a thing for long hair, especially when it's free and wild."

"Wouldn't it be a little obvious what I'm trying to do?"

"Men don't care, they just like the finished product." Brooke worked to stand up from the sofa, then paused as the baby began moving around.

Laurel came over and gave her a hand. "Are you okay?"

"Yeah, little Christopher is practicing football or soccer." She rubbed her stomach, loving the feel of her child inside her. "Maybe he'll be a bronc rider like Grandpa Rory."

Laurel laid her hand on Brooke's stomach and smiled. "Yep, definitely a bronc rider."

Once the baby quieted, Brooke turned to her sister. "Okay, back to you. Are you saying you want Kase's attention?"

"I don't know." Laurel threw up her hands. "I haven't exactly been on the right track when it comes to men."

"Then just do it for yourself. I've watched you work so hard, sis, day in and day out."

"What if Kase leaves again, like before?"

"And what if he stays? People can change careers. Trent did when he retired from the army and came back here to ranch. Even when this place had bad memories, with his brother's death and his parents' divorce, he came back and made a life here. We're building a life together."

Brooke took Laurel's hand, praying her sister would find happiness. "Now Kase has returned to work with his dad. Maybe he'll decide he wants what was right here all along."

"I'm worried that Kase's only staying here because his in-laws want to take Addy. He might head back to Denver to practice law again once the custody is resolved."

"Then convince him to stay here," Brooke told her. "Make Kase see what's right in front of him."

Laurel finally smiled. These past several months had been wonderful, having her sister to share everything with. "Okay, start working your miracles."

She got up and her phone rang. She pulled it out of her pocket and looked at the unfamiliar number and no name.

"Who is it?" Brooke asked.

"I don't know. I don't recognize the number." She punched the screen to talk. "Hello? Hello?"

She disconnected. "No answer. Shoot, I was hoping it was Kase about Gus."

Brooke took her sister's hand and they headed up the stairs. "This is going to be a girls' day, a makeover and a trip to see Coralee, and no thoughts of men." They both laughed, knowing that wasn't true.

KASE PACED THE hospital's waiting room. He glanced at the clock on the wall. Gus had been in surgery for nearly three hours and he couldn't help but wonder if there had been complications. Unable to sit still any longer, he walked down the hall to the large picture window. The sunlight made him squint as he looked out at the majestic Rocky Mountains.

In the past year his life had been in turmoil, from his crumbling marriage, his lost career and his battle for custody of Addy. Coming back to Hidden Springs had been the best decision, but until all the issues got resolved he wouldn't be able to find any solace.

After years of feeling disconnected, he was trying to rebuild a relationship with his father. The once-a-month courtesy phone calls didn't count.

When Kase had left here for college, he thought he knew everything. He hadn't needed his father's advice and told Gus so. How he wished he could take back the angry words. Now he wanted nothing more than to have the old man's guidance.

An overwhelming rush of emotions had him blinking back tears. "Please, God, don't let anything happen to him," he breathed. "I need him, Addy needs him."

His thoughts turned to his daughter, and he wondered how she was doing. He knew Laurel would keep Addy distracted, but the child had already lost her mother, and she was scared she'd lose Papa Gus, too.

He thought about how Laurel held his daughter, the loving touches. How he envied the attention the woman gave so freely to his child, and wished he could share in that affection. But he had no business expecting anything from Laurel, especially after the way he'd left her. And the crazy notion of a marriage to her would help his chances for custody. Even if he'd said it in jest, he had no right to even suggest the possibility.

His life was a mess, but he still wanted Laurel, and it was quickly turning into a need to be with her, to want to share things with her. Maybe building a life with her wasn't so far-fetched. He did know she would have to forgive him for the past before they could think of building a future.

"Mr. Rawlins?"

Kase turned to find the doctor dressed in green scrubs. "Yes, Doctor? How is my dad?"

A smile appeared on the man's face. "He did fine. He's in recovery, already awake and wanting to leave."

His chest tightened as a burst of laughter erupted. Over his professional life, he'd always been able to lock away his emotions. Not today. "I'm sorry." He wiped at the tears in his eyes. "It's just so overwhelming."

"No need to apologize," the doctor told him. "Gus is your father. He's just had major surgery."

They started walking down the hall, and Kase asked, "But he's okay?"

The doctor nodded. "Yes. He needs pain meds now, but with physical therapy he should be walking fine."

They walked through the surgical unit and into recovery. Kase paused on seeing Gus flat on the bed. He didn't hesitate as he went to his side. He took hold of his father's hand and squeezed it. "Dad, it's me, Kase."

Gus blinked his eyes and gave a lopsided grin. "Hi, son."

He smiled back. "How are you feeling?"

"Like they tried to rip off my leg, but the pretty nurse gave me some kind of medicine. Now I…feel…good. You want to take me home?"

Kase looked at the nurse and she said, "It's the pain medication. They all get a little silly. Your father is doing fine." She leaned down to the patient. "Gus, we're going to take you to your room in a little while. And feed you some of the wonderful hospital food you've heard about. Best Jell-O in town."

"As long as you'll serve it to me."

"Of course." The nurse looked over to Kase. "Why don't you go and call your family with the news. By then we'll have Gus settled in his room."

After promising his dad he'd be right back, Kase went back into the waiting area. Even though it had been only a few weeks since he'd reconnected with Laurel, she was the first person he wanted to tell the news. What he'd left behind in search of that so-called perfect life. His thoughts turned to Laurel. It seemed that everything he'd been looking for was right here all this time.

LATER THAT EVENING, Kase pulled into the Quinns' driveway. He was exhausted, but he needed to get his daughter and take her home to bed. He climbed the steps and knocked on the back door, then walked inside.

"Hello?" he called before he went into the kitchen. He found the Quinn family seated around the table.

"Daddy, you're here." Addy got off her chair and came running. "Is Papa okay?"

He lifted her into his arms and inhaled that wonderful child scent. "He's doing fine, sweetie."

"Does he have a big bandage?"

"Yes, he does. He said to tell you he loves you and can't wait to see you. How about we go tomorrow?"

Her blue eyes widened. "I get to go to the hospital?"

Kase nodded. "We can't stay long, but I think he'll feel better if he sees you."

"Can we take him flowers, too? Mimi says sometimes when people are sick it's nice to take them flowers."

"Sure, we'll take him flowers." He glanced around the

table to see everyone watching them, except for Diane, who went to the cupboard and got him a plate.

"Now, you sit down and eat," Diane said. "I'm sure you're plenty hungry."

"I really hate to interrupt your meal." His stomach growled, and his daughter laughed.

"Daddy, I think you got a bear in your tummy."

He set her down in her seat. "I guess I wouldn't mind some supper. Thank you."

He looked across the table at Laurel. Her light blond hair was down and her usually scrubbed-clean face had a little color, especially her eyes. She looked beautiful. "Hello, Laurel."

"Hi, Kase."

"Thank you for watching Addy today."

She nodded. "You're welcome. We're glad that Gus is doing so well. Does he need anything?"

He brushed his hand over Addy's blond hair. "Just this little one."

"Best medicine ever," Rory said.

"I think it'll do both of them good," he said as Diane set down a plate filled with sliced beef, mashed potatoes and gravy. "Thank you, Diane, this looks wonderful."

"It tastes really good, Daddy. But you better eat or you don't get any dessert. Mimi and me made an apple pie. So clean your plate."

Laughter rang out. "Not a problem."

He enjoyed the family surroundings in the oversize kitchen. Funny how he once thought this was so boring. He looked across the table at Laurel and locked on those mesmerizing green eyes. He felt a tightening in his stomach, and his fingers itched to touch those wild curls. Oh, he was far from bored.

He felt Addy's hand on his arm, shaking it. "Daddy. Daddy."

He tore his gaze away and looked at his daughter. "What, sweetheart?"

"Brooke and Laurel and me went to see Miss Coralee today. She lives with a lot of old people. And sometimes she couldn't remember my name, but Laurel told me it was because she forgets things."

Addy wrinkled her nose. "I had to tell her my name three times. That's okay because she was nice to me, even if she called me Laurel." Addy smiled. "Then we left and went to lunch. It was girls' day, no boys allowed." His daughter giggled. "We had a lot of fun."

Kase looked at Laurel. "No men, huh? I hope that rule isn't every day."

"No," Addy assured him. "But girls need time to get all pretty just for themselves, and they don't need men around."

Rory coughed, Diane tried to hide her smile and Laurel's cheeks flamed. She said, "Remind me never to tell this little one any secrets."

AN HOUR LATER, after delicious apple pie, Addy and Diane went upstairs to get her overnight bag. Rory poured himself a cup of coffee, excused himself and went into his office.

Laurel was at the sink finishing up some of the pans that didn't go into the dishwasher.

Kase went to her. "I should be doing those. You've worked all day and took care of Addy."

She didn't look up as she quickly rinsed off the platter and placed it in the drainer. "I'm finished." She grabbed the towel.

He didn't move away. He found he liked being close to

her, feeling her warmth, inhaling her intoxicating scent. He hadn't had this kind of reaction to a woman in a very long time.

"You've done so much, thank you. Addy has had so much fun staying here."

Laurel shrugged as she wiped her hands on a towel. "We did have a fun girls' day. Brooke is about to deliver her baby soon and it's time we got to spend together." She looked at him. "I hope you didn't mind us taking Addy to see Coralee."

He shook his head. "It's good that she spends time with other people. I probably should have her in preschool so she can socialize with other kids her age."

"That's a good idea. But you've been a little busy with Gus. I could ask Melody, the receptionist at work, where she takes her two kids."

"Thank you. I didn't send her before because she'd been with too many babysitters and Gus wanted to get to know his granddaughter. But she needs to be with kids her own age. At least a few mornings a week, especially with Dad laid up at the house during his rehab."

She turned back to the sink and began to wipe off the counter. "Have you found someone to come out and work with him?"

He caught another whiff of her soft powdery scent. His gaze went to her new-looking pair of jeans, and the way they caressed her nicely rounded bottom. He lost his train of thought for a moment.

"No, but I have several names that I need to call." He pulled the list out of his shirt pocket. "Do you know any of these therapists?"

She took the list from him. Her teeth bit down on her lower lip in concentration and his pulse began to race. "I know Darcy Mason. She comes out here to ride sometimes.

Her husband, Matt, is a firefighter in town. She also volunteers at the medical care facility where Coralee resides."

"Maybe I'll try her first."

Laurel gave back the paper and saw Kase staring at her. "Is something wrong? You're looking at me funny."

He smiled. "I like your hair down. I remember you used to wear it like that when we were in school."

She was uncomfortable with his attention. "I work all day with horses. It's easier to tie back."

He reached out and touched the curls. "Soft. So pretty."

She swallowed hard, trying to rid the dryness in her throat. "Thank you." He'd moved closer and she wasn't sure what to do. Suddenly her phone rang, causing her to jump.

"Excuse me." She punched the answer button. "Hello?"

There was a long silence, then she heard a soft "Laurel."

She froze, recognizing the voice, then turned away. "If this is who I think it is, be man enough to talk to me."

"I'm sorry" was the only answer she got, then the line was dead. She cursed and looked at the number. Redialed it, but no one answered.

"Are you okay?" Kase asked.

She shook her head. "I'm pretty sure that was Jack."

"The man you were supposed to marry?"

She added, "And the creep who stole from my parents and Trent."

Kase took her phone and looked at the number. "It's a Denver prefix."

"We went to Denver last fall, trying to find him."

"Are you positive that's who was on the phone?"

She shrugged, quickly losing her confidence. "He only said my name, 'Laurel,' and then 'I'm sorry.'" She looked at him. "Should I call the police?"

"And say what? You got a call that might be your

ex-fiancé." He got a pen and paper off the counter and wrote down the number, then pocketed the information. "Let me see if I can find out whom it belongs to. Don't say anything until I learn more."

He paused and reached out and touched her cheek. "I'm sorry he hurt you, Laurel."

She glanced away. "It's okay, I'm over Jack. He was one of the mistakes in my life."

"Seems we've all made those." He had so many regrets, he was afraid to start the list, because right on top would be Laurel.

Chapter Seven

The next week, Gus had come home from the hospital, but since he wasn't ready to climb stairs just yet, Kase had moved him into the den on the main floor.

Equipment had been rented for his therapy, and Darcy Mason had been hired to work with Gus five days a week. Luckily, his dad hadn't complained, not about being confined to the house, or about the strenuous exercises Darcy had put him through. Right now, all his dad cared about was being with Addy and his horses.

Kase also knew his daughter needed more interaction with kids her own age, so he'd enrolled Addy into Saint Theresa Preschool in town. At first Addy had been nervous about leaving him, but once she'd arrived at the school and seen all the other kids, she agreed to give it a try. She quickly began to make friends. Best news, Laurel had offered to pick her up on the days she worked for the accountant and bring Addy home. Plus she could also help out with the horses.

Today was one of those days, and he found he was anxious to see her. Crazy, huh? He'd just seen her two days ago, but that didn't seem to matter. He told himself that the reason was because he had some news about her mysterious phone call. The way his insides churned and the restlessness he'd been feeling, he knew it was more. This was all about seeing Laurel.

"Staring out the window isn't going to bring her here any faster."

Kase turned to see his father leaning on his walker. Darn, the man could always read him. "Shouldn't you be in bed?"

"No, I need to walk around to help with circulation. Hurts like the blazes since Darcy's torture session this morning, but it's getting better." He grimaced as he moved across the kitchen. "That girl should be in the military. She could whip our troops into shape."

Gus nodded toward the window. "Laurel's truck just pulled into the drive. Go ask her to come in. I'd like her to check on Romeo for me."

"I need to talk to her about something…private."

His father raised an eyebrow. "Then go."

Kase stepped outside in the warm sunlight just as Laurel climbed out of the truck. She waved to him as she walked to the back door to unbuckle his daughter.

Kase went to help. "Here, let me get her. She's too heavy for you."

"You're kidding, right? Have you seen the horses I work with? Addy is a lightweight."

"I'm big," the child said. "Hi, Daddy."

"Hi, sweetie. How was your day?"

He lifted her out of the seat. "I played with Chelsea, but she was mean and didn't want Kelly to play with us, too. Kelly cried so I hugged her and we played together. And Chelsea got a time-out for not sharing."

His heart swelled with pride. "I'm glad you were nice."

"I don't like people who are mean." She turned sad. "Now Kelly is my new friend. And if Chelsea can be nice, we'll play with her, too."

"Good girl." He set her down. "Go inside and see to Papa Gus. He's been waiting all morning for you."

"I drew a picture for him." Holding the paper up, the child ran off.

After the screen door shut, Kase turned to Laurel. She was dressed in a dark slim skirt, giving him a glimpse of her long, shapely legs while the cream-colored silky blouse caressed the curve of her breasts. His thoughts wandered until he directed his attention to her face. Light makeup enhanced her eyes, and he loved that she wore her hair down. "I like your hair that way," he said.

She smiled shyly. "Thank you."

"If you have some time, Gus would like to speak with you. But before you go inside, I need to discuss something with you."

She blinked those big green eyes at him. "Sure."

"It's about the phone call you got the other day. I had the number checked out. We got a location. It was from a pay phone outside a Denver restaurant. There's no way to trace it back to Jack."

She sighed. "Of course, that would make it too easy to find him."

"Look, Laurel. I know it's disappointing, but I'm more concerned that this guy might try to contact you again, or even come back to see you."

Laurel clenched her fists. "If Jack does, I have a few things to say to him before I call the sheriff."

He frowned. "Calling the sheriff is a good idea, but not confronting him. This guy might not have a police record, but he stole money from you, and he has connections with some pretty sleazy characters. And that worries me because the word is Jack owes them money, too. And if they find out about your connection to him, they might come after you for it."

She studied him. "How did you find this out?"

"I have a great PI, Clark Johnson. I asked him to do some investigating. He talked with some of the neighbors at Aldrich's last address. Seems there are some rough-looking characters also looking for him."

"How much did this investigator of yours cost?"

Kase knew she would want to pay him. "He's on retainer with the law firm."

"But you don't work there anymore."

"Let's just say he owed me a favor."

"My dad and Trent already had Jack investigated last year. We already knew he was a gambler and needed money to pay back debts."

He had a feeling Jack's problems were much more than a few debts. "Just be careful, Laurel. Aldrich might be a two-bit hustler, but he's on the run. That makes him dangerous. So if he calls again, let me know."

"Kase, I don't want you to get involved in my mess. It was my mistake to believe Jack, and it cost my family."

Did she truly believe this was all her fault? "This guy deceived everyone, Laurel, including Trent and your dad."

She avoided his gaze. "I just feel so stupid for falling for his lies."

He touched her cheek and made her look at him. When those emerald eyes glistened, he found himself mesmerized by her. "When we fall in love, we aren't always smart. You loved the guy."

She sighed. "Who said love had anything to do with it?" She turned and headed toward the house, leaving Kase shaking his head and wondering why the hell she had been going to marry the guy then.

THIRTY MINUTES LATER, Laurel had gone to the Rawlinses' barn to check Gus's horses. He might have only a half dozen, but they were all quality quarter horses. Gus had asked her to exercise Romeo, and she couldn't refuse. After she changed into a pair of jeans and boots she kept in her truck, she took the roan stallion out into the corral. She climbed into the saddle and began to ride him around the arena, and slowly the tension from her day, and the disappointing news from Kase, began to disappear on this magnificent horse.

Not ten minutes later, Kase came out of the barn with Honor's Promise. The big chestnut mare pranced excitedly as if showing off. Once she settled down, Kase rode her toward the gate. After he opened it, he motioned for Laurel to join him on the other side.

She hesitated, then nodded toward the mare. "How has she been around the stallions?"

"Ignoring them mostly."

That wasn't a good sign. "You think she's pregnant?"

"I'm not an expert so I had the vet come out. Besides an exam, he also did an ultrasound." He gave that cocky smile of his. "Looks like we're officially going to be parents." He wheeled his horse around. "Come on, let's go for a ride."

She followed once she closed her mouth, which she'd opened in surprise. Was he happy about the foal? She was. This could help build her stallion's reputation. She smiled. This was turning out to be a good day.

Once the gate was shut, she took off in a canter. Kase caught up to her, then led her along a path. Since she didn't know where she was, she followed him. That was very enjoyable. He might be a lawyer now, but he still looked good on horseback. Relaxed in the saddle, he held the reins lax, but in command. She couldn't help but remember those teenage days when they'd ridden together. There were so many places they could find for privacy.

Once they got to a clearing, Kase gave her a sideways glance. "Let's pick up the pace," he called.

She smiled. "What about Gus and Addy?"

"Dad knows we went riding, and he has my cell number."

"Okay, then." Pushing her hat down on her head, she put her heels into the horse's sides and the animal shot off. They galloped across the high grass as a herd of cattle grazed in the distance. She felt the cool spring air against her face, and the powerful stallion moving under her. There was nothing better. She glanced at the man beside her. Well, she could think of a few things. She turned away from the temptation and raced across the field.

Soon they came upon a grove of trees beside the creek, and Kase slowed his mare, then he began to walk her alongside the water. Once in a clearing, he stopped and climbed down. "Let's give them a rest before we start back."

"Good idea." Laurel swung her leg over the saddle and slid to the ground. Holding the reins, she led Romeo to the stream, where he dipped his head and began to drink.

Kase did the same. "Does this look familiar?"

Laurel sat down on the rocky edge, but she didn't have to look around to remember. She'd thought about this spot so many times, replayed that last day Kase had brought her here.

"It's been over ten years, and the trees are bigger, but yes, I remember. You used to bring me here when we'd go riding." And where she'd given herself to the boy she loved and thought loved her, too.

Kase joined her on the ground. "I wish there were only good times to remember here. It's hard, since I can only think about the last time we were here."

She placed her chin on her raised knees, recalling

that day when he told her he didn't want her any longer. "Gosh, it can't be ten years ago. Sometimes, it seems like yesterday." She finally looked at him. "When you came home from college that first time, you seemed different. You seemed to have turned into someone I didn't know."

He looked away. "Yeah, a semester of college and I thought I knew everything. I made new friends, was pledging a fraternity. I thought I was too cool to be from Hidden Springs."

He turned back to her, his expression serious. "I did so many things wrong, Laurel. I'll regret until my dying day how much I hurt you."

She hated that their breakup still hurt her. "We were both so young, Kase. And a long-distance relationship wouldn't have worked anyway." She looked out to the water again. "It was for the best. You're forgiven for being a teenage boy."

"It still wasn't right, Laurel." He sighed. "I can't tell you how many times I wanted to call you, just to talk."

She blinked at the tears, working hard to keep them from falling. The last thing she wanted was for Kase to see the pain he'd caused her. And that it still bothered her. She put on a smile and looked at him. "You should have. I would have liked to know how you were doing. It's funny because our parents weren't exactly friends back then, or I would have asked Gus about you. I'm glad they got everything resolved with the land dispute. Now they're good neighbors. And you and Addy are our neighbors, too."

He leaned in closer and she inhaled his familiar scent. "How can you be so generous?"

"What do you want me to do, Kase? Yell at you, tell you that you broke my heart? Of course you did, you were my first boyfriend, my first love. I gave myself to you right here." Oh, God. She looked down at the soft grass, and she flashed back to how his kisses had her crazy, causing a fire and a desire that she'd never found with any other man.

He turned toward her. "If it's any consolation, Laurel, I regret pushing you out of my life. I struggled with so many things all those years, and I found my career was all I could manage well. And when I did begin to have success, I married someone who I thought would help me. Instead, I couldn't give her what she needed."

She raised her head. "Are you saying you married for your career?"

He shook his head. "At first, I was enamored by Johanna. She was breathtakingly beautiful, we had a physical attraction, but there wasn't much else, no friendship, no shared interests. Everything about her was superficial. All she cared about was a social life, and getting her parents to love her."

He tore at a piece of grass. "When Mom and Dad didn't give it to her, she wanted my undivided attention. I had to work. Her father, Ben Chappell, insisted I put in a lot of hours for the firm. Bring in clients. Then Johanna thought a baby would keep me close to her."

Kase glanced away. "I still let work keep me from home. Because Addy was so young, I didn't think she would miss me. I thought Johanna and Addy needed the money and nice things more than me. It took a tragedy to make me realize I was wrong."

"Oh, Kase, I'm so sorry. But you are with Addy now, and she adores you."

"I don't ever want her to feel unloved again. That's why I'll do anything to keep her safe and secure, keep her from living in a sterile environment with her grand-parents."

She finally smiled. "You might have made mistakes in life, but you're a good dad, Kase. No one can take Addy from you."

He took her hands in his and squeezed them. "That means a lot to me, Laurel. You still mean a lot to me. That's the one thing that hasn't changed over the years." He leaned forward, and Laurel panicked but couldn't seem to pull away. When he brushed his lips over hers, she sucked in a long breath.

"Kase, this isn't a good idea."

"I disagree. It's the best idea I've had in a long time." His mouth closed over hers.

Kase had to be crazy, tempting himself with this woman, but even knowing he couldn't start anything right now didn't stop him. He pulled her close, trying to ease that gnawing in his gut.

Laurel felt wonderful in his arms, her breasts pressed against his chest. The feel of her mouth under his was both erotic and sweet at the same time. He loved those soft sounds she made when his tongue slipped past her lips to taste her.

He groaned this time and tightened his hold. Oh, God, he wanted her. Her arms moved up his chest and circled his neck as she angled her head to deepen the kiss. A kiss he never wanted to end. Finally he tore his mouth away but didn't release her.

"Wow. That was just as incredible as I remembered." His hands continued to move up and down her back, aching to press closer, to feel her body against his. To lay her down on the sweetgrass and make love to her.

When Romeo whinnied, Laurel pulled out of Kase's

embrace, then stood. "Still, that doesn't mean it was a good idea. Besides, our lives are far from settled."

He looked at her. "So I just pretend I don't have feelings for you?"

A WEEK LATER in the afternoon at the Bucking Q Ranch, Laurel sat on Ruby Ridge and cantered the mare around the arena and began the reining routine with a figure eight.

After warming up, she began the first pattern with a fast circle at a near gallop and then with a change of direction began the loping circle. She marveled at the horse's response to her commands, making her look good.

Ruby began along the side of the arena, picking up speed into a gallop, then suddenly the horse slid to a stop in the center of the arena and backed up in a straight line.

"Oh, good girl," Laurel cheered as the mare performed perfectly. She saw Chet on the fence railing shouting his approval. She waved and continued on. After another twenty minutes she and the horse were ready to call it a day.

Laurel climbed down and walked the animal to the barn. She paused when she saw Kase leaning against the railing.

Her heart began to race on seeing him for the first time since their kiss. She'd been avoiding him when she'd dropped off Addy. Even when the little girl would invite her inside, Laurel had made excuses to keep from seeing Kase. She couldn't let him get close enough to hurt her again. Besides, her goal now was to pay back her parents, and she couldn't let Kase Rawlins distract her from that.

Problem was, she'd already fallen in love with Addy and Gus, and hated not seeing them.

She continued to walk Ruby to the barn and Kase

came to her. "How long are you going to avoid me, Laurel?"

She handed Ruby off to Chet. Once he took the animal into the barn, she said, "I've been busy, Kase."

"You're not a very good liar," he challenged.

She turned to face him, all six feet one inch of the gorgeous man. "I'm trying to run a business here. Not all of us are independently wealthy."

Seeing his hurt look, she wished she could take her words back.

"Whoever gave you that information better check their facts. I'm not poor yet, but if I have to keep paying my lawyer's bill, I will be soon." He took a step closer. "So you don't have to wonder any longer, my wife was rich, not me. Johanna's money is in trust for Addy. Not that I would, but I can't touch it. Sorry I interrupted your training, it won't happen again." He took off down the center aisle of the barn.

"Kase…" She hurried after him. "I'm sorry. I shouldn't have said that. I was just angry…"

"Because I kissed you and you felt something?"

"No! Yes… I did. But we're not teenagers anymore."

"No, we're adults. You're not married and I'm not married. What's so wrong if I kiss you?"

She could get hurt. "What about your custody issues with Addy?"

He ran his hand through his sandy-colored hair. "That's all I've been thinking about, and Dad, of course."

He didn't act anything like the self-assured man she'd seen the past few weeks. "What happened?"

He looked at her. "Why do you think something happened?"

"For a lawyer, your mannerisms give a lot away." She tried to make light of the situation.

"I'm not in the courtroom. I thought I was talking to a friend."

"You are. What happened? Is it Gus?"

He shook his head. "I have a custody hearing in two days."

"Whoa, that was fast."

He nodded. "I think Ben is pulling some strings to get this in front of a judge. I don't want to take Addy back to Denver, and with Dad still unable to get around, I need to ask…"

"You want me to stay with them while you're gone?"

"I don't have anyone else to ask. If I hire a professional babysitter, both Dad and Addy would throw a fit."

"They would throw more than that."

She caught his smile, and her heart raced.

"Seriously, Kase, I can stay with them while you're gone. How long?"

"I wouldn't ask if it weren't for Addy. Dad would probably be okay by himself, but if something happened, like if he fell…"

Laurel reached out and touched his arm. "It's only a few days, Kase. The most important thing is you handle this case for your daughter."

He shook his head. "I don't even want to think about it. I don't know why Ben and Judith want Addy anyway. They never spent any time with her. Why now?"

She hated seeing him so worried. "I'm sorry, Kase, that you have to go through this. Worse, I hate that Addy has to go through it. When do you want me to move in?"

"Tomorrow night. I'll leave at dawn the next morning. Dad's room is vacant, since he's been sleeping downstairs during his recovery."

She'd be in the same house with him. "Of course." She glanced away. "I'll get Chet to take over my training for a few days. I still have to work two mornings this week, but since Addy will be in school… Will Gus be okay by himself while I'm at the office?"

"Yes, he has therapy, and he'll get around all right by himself. I just don't want him responsible for a four-year-old."

"I'll have Mom stop by while I'm at work, or maybe Dad."

He shook his head. "That's not necessary, Laurel."

"Are you kidding? Mom will probably drop by with a pile of food. I won't have to cook."

He laughed. "I'll leave money so you can bring home food from town. That way you don't have to cook."

"So you think I can't cook?"

"I couldn't care less if you can or not. I just don't want any extra work for you."

She smiled. "That's nice of you, but I'm Diane Quinn's daughter. I was cooking before I went to school."

"I figured you could." His gray gaze locked on hers and his hand reached out and touched her cheek. She knew she needed to back away, but the pull of the man was too strong. That she ached for his touch made her angry. She was in big trouble, but she couldn't seem to stop herself.

Chapter Eight

The next evening, Kase sat at the kitchen table across from Gus and Laurel, eating Addy's favorite meal, spaghetti. All the while his daughter chatted away about her day at school, excited that Laurel was spending the night.

He was excited, too, but for a whole different reason.

"Child, slow down," Gus said. "Let Laurel eat her supper. You have two days to share all your news."

"It's okay," Laurel told him. "I'm glad Addy likes her new school and that she's making friends."

The child nodded, causing her blond curls to bounce. "I do. Lots and lots, but you're still my bestest friend."

Laurel stroked the child's hair. "That's so sweet, Addy. Thank you."

Kase was touched at Laurel's open affection. Although he was happy his daughter had female attention, what would happen when Laurel wasn't around all the time? Would his daughter be devastated again?

And how would he feel if Laurel found another man?

A man who didn't come with baggage, or a man who wasn't fighting a custody battle that would put any potential woman in his life under intense scrutiny. The right thing to do would be to keep her out of his mess. Yet he couldn't dismiss his growing feelings for her.

He watched the pretty blonde whom he'd loved once, then hurt when he pushed her aside.

She looked across the table, and her smile faded away. "Is something the matter?"

Where do I begin? He shook his head. "I just want some more sauce."

Kase scooted his chair back, went to the stove and stirred the spaghetti sauce, then poured more on his plate. He turned to see Laurel bending over toward Addy. Her hair was tied back, but some curls had escaped the band. There wasn't any makeup on her face, revealing a dusting of freckles across her nose. Her lips were naturally pink and full. The memory of their kiss had him wanting to taste her again.

"Son, you okay?"

He glanced at his dad's odd look.

"I'm fine." He made his way back to his chair and began to eat.

Laurel took a drink of her iced tea, then asked, "What time are you leaving in the morning?"

"Five a.m. I'm driving, so I want to make sure I have plenty of time."

He glanced at Addy, grateful she was happy twirling spaghetti on her fork. "Are you going to be gone a long, long time?" his daughter asked.

"No, sweetie. Only a couple days for business."

"But I thought Papa Gus's horsies were your new business."

"They are, but I have to go back to Denver and see about selling our old house." It was a complete fib. If he had time, he would check in with the Realtor.

"'Kay." She shook her head. "I don't like that house."

Her statement caught him off guard. "Why?"

"It was scary there."

"Scary how?" he asked.

"I got locked in the closet when I was playing dollies. I cried and cried...but Mommy didn't come find me for a really long time." She shook her head. "I didn't play in there anymore."

Kase clenched his fists against his jeans. Surely Johanna hadn't locked their daughter inside? He looked at Addy and saw a tear run down her cheek. He stood, went around the table and pulled his daughter out of her chair.

"Oh, Addy, don't cry." He cuddled the tiny child in his arms. "You're never going to get locked in a closet again. I promise. In fact, when I get home, I'm taking all the locks off the doors."

Addy raised her head and wiped her tears. "Really?"

He felt the sting of his own tears. "For you, I'd do anything. I love you, sweetie."

"I love you, too, Daddy. I miss you when you go away."

Guilt washed over him as he recalled all the times he spent away from her. "I'll be back soon and I'll call you before you go to bed tomorrow night."

She rewarded him with a big smile. This thirty-seven-pound child had stolen his heart. He was grateful she was giving him a second chance to be her father.

"Daddy, could we watch a movie tonight?"

He glanced at the clock to see it was nearly seven. "It's getting late and you need a bath."

"I can give her a bath," Laurel suggested as she stood up from the table.

Addy grinned. "With bubbles?"

"If you don't make a mess and hurry up," Kase said as Addy darted around the table. "Papa and I will do the dishes."

Laurel took the child's hand. "I bet we're finished with our bath before you finish the dishes," she challenged.

"Yeah," Addy said.

Kase couldn't help but smile at his two girls. "It's a bet."

He watched the happy twosome hurry out of the kitchen, then he sat back down at the maple table with his father.

Gus shook his head. "Those two are really something."

There was no doubt Gus liked that Laurel was around so much. "Yeah. I don't want to disappoint either one of them again."

His father studied him. "You won't, son. Just don't walk away from what you really want."

WITH THE DISHES FINISHED, Gus settled in front of the television and Kase went upstairs to see what was taking the girls so long. Once he got to the bathroom door, he heard the giggling and splashing.

He smiled, loving his daughter's joyful sounds. He opened the door a crack and peaked inside. He froze when he saw Addy's reflection in the mirror. She was barely visible in the pile of bubbles, and she wasn't alone, either. On the other end of the claw-foot tub, also buried in suds, was Laurel.

Her blond curls were piled on her head, exposing her long neck and shoulders, and the top of her breasts. He swallowed the sudden dryness in his throat as a need stirred in his gut. Dear God, she was beautiful.

Laurel couldn't help but smile at the antics of this child. She loved her honest approach to everything, and her innocence. Although she hadn't planned to take a shared bath with the four-year-old, Addy convinced her it would be fun.

"Will my chest get big like yours?" The child looked down at her own flat chest.

Strange, but Laurel didn't feel the least bit self-conscious about the question. "Yes, and one day when you have a baby, you'll need to feed her or him."

"You mean like horsies do?"

"Yes, like when the mare feeds her foal."

Addy smiled. "Are you going to have a baby someday?"

The familiar yearning stirred in her chest. "I hope so." She would love to have a child like Addy, and a good man in her life. "Just not real soon."

"But why not? I know, you can marry Daddy."

Before Laurel could recover from the shock of Addy's suggestion, there was a loud knock on the door. "Hey, are you girls in there?"

Startled at the sound of Kase's voice, they both cried out in surprise. "Don't come in, we're in the tub," Laurel said, not expecting to see Kase. A thrill shot through her body, her breathing suddenly labored, thinking about him coming in.

"Yeah, Daddy, we're naked."

Laurel couldn't help but laugh. "Yeah, so no boys allowed." She sank deeper into the bubbles along with Addy.

It had been a long time since she let herself go and have fun. She glanced down at the sweet child, knowing she wanted her as much as she wanted her father.

LAUREL HEARD HER NAME, and she rolled over in the bed to read the clock on the table. Five a.m. She dropped her head back on the pillow. Kase was gone.

"Laurel." Hearing her name whispered again, she sat up and saw the shadowy figure by the door. "Kase?"

She threw the blanket back and got out of bed. Dressed in her pajama bottoms and T-shirt, she went to Kase standing in the doorway. A lamp from down the hall silhouetted the man.

"Sorry to wake you, but I wanted to see you once more before I left."

"I'm glad you did." Her gaze took him in. He was dressed in a pair of dark suit pants and a white shirt, a loose tie around his neck. "I want to wish you a safe trip. Be careful driving."

"I will. You be careful not to overwork. I only want you to keep an eye on Dad and Addy. I don't want her to run you ragged."

He leaned forward and she could feel his breath against her face. She inhaled the subtle scent of his aftershave.

She brushed her hair back nervously. "We'll be fine. She needs to be distracted so as not to worry about you. I'll take her by the Bucking Q so she can see my mom while I check on my horses."

"What would I do without you?" His gaze locked on hers, causing her heart to race. She felt her nipples harden and she crossed her arms to hide the fact.

"You would have found someone else to help out, Kase. But I'm glad I'm here for you. The important thing is you focus on resolving this custody mess."

"I know. I can't move on until I know she won't be taken away from me." He sighed. "Laurel, I can't tell you how much I've enjoyed spending time with you. When I get back, I want to see…"

She leaned forward and brushed her mouth against his. She couldn't handle listening to promises he might not be able to keep. "You need to get going and get this custody resolved first."

He nodded, then reached for her. "Then I need something more to keep me going." He bent his head and captured her mouth in a searing kiss. She couldn't help but respond as incredible feelings raced through her. Of course, Kase had always had that effect on her.

His tongue slipped into her mouth, moving against hers, causing her to whimper. Her breasts tingled with need when he pulled her to his chest. Her arms went around his neck, and he deepened the kiss. Okay, she was crazy. If anything, she would give Kase something to think about while he was gone.

He finally tore his mouth away. "Damn, woman. How do you expect me to leave now?"

She froze. He noticed her tension, and when she started to pull back, he stopped her.

"We're definitely talking once this is settled, Laurel," he whispered against her mouth. "There are so many things I want to say to you, but now isn't the time."

She nodded, then gave him a slight shove. "Then you need to go win this suit. I'm not going anywhere."

He kissed her once more, turned and walked away as she felt a sense of gloom rush over her.

Don't make me any promises.

AT EIGHT FORTY that morning, Kase pulled into the parking structure at the courthouse. His lawyer, Sam Gerrard, met him on the third floor. Sam had gone to college with him. He was built more like a linebacker dressed in a polyester suit, instead of a designer label like Armani. His blond hair was a little long, and his smile was big and confident. As much as Kase wanted to be a big corporate lawyer, Sam went in the opposite direction, working for the underdogs. Family law, with much of his service pro bono work. One thing for sure, the man was good at his job.

Together they headed to Judge Harold Steffen's chambers. Even knowing this was routine for an informal hearing, Kase couldn't help but worry. It only got worse once they walked through the doors of the large plush office. He froze. On one side of the dark-paneled room, in front of the large desk, sat Ben and Judith Chappell and their lawyer, the firm's partner and custody lawyer, Charles Hannett. Ben brought the big guns and that worried Kase.

What was the man's reasoning for this? And then there was the attractive Judith Kirsch Chappell. She turned around, revealing her perfectly made-up face. She blinked as if he wasn't worth her time to even acknowledge him. Even though she'd never been crazy about him as a son-in-law, wouldn't she at least ask about Addy?

Never an attentive grandmother, Judith spent her days at the country club with her bridge tournaments and social events. There was never time for her daughter, Johanna, or Addy.

Suddenly the severity of today hit Kase and he had to swallow down his panic. He leaned toward his lawyer and in a low voice said, "I can't figure out what's going on here. Ben is out for blood and I don't know why."

"He can't touch your character, Kase. You have nothing in your background that could possibly keep you from raising your daughter."

Kase wanted to believe his lawyer. "I don't like the fact that the presiding judge is a friend of Ben's. Harold Steffen and he golf together."

Sam nodded. "I'm going to request he not handle this case because of a conflict of interest."

The chamber door opened and the judge walked in. Everyone stood as he took a seat behind his desk.

"Have a seat, gentlemen and ladies." He nodded to Judith and the female court reporter. Kase and his lawyer sat in the two chairs opposite the Chappells.

The white-haired judge was in his sixties, short in stature and unable to hide the extra forty pounds under his robe. He glanced down at the file on his desk and read the case number for the court reporter. "Benjamin and Judith Chappell versus Kase James Rawlins for the custody of minor female child Addison Marie Rawlins."

Sam stood. "Your Honor, in view of this situation, your knowing and socializing with the Chappells, I feel that it's in the interest of my client that you recuse yourself from this case."

The judge leaned back in his chair and steepled his fingers as if thinking over the matter. "I know both Mr. Chappell and Mr. Rawlins, Mr. Gerrard. They both have been in my court several times, and so far this is an informal hearing. I'm here to see if there is any validity to this case. For now, your request is denied, Mr. Gerrard."

Sam sat down.

The judge looked at Ben's lawyer and nodded. "Let's begin."

Charles Hannett stood. "I'm representing Ben and Judith Chappell for the custody of their granddaughter, Addison Marie, under the grounds that Kase Rawlins is unfit to raise her."

Sam stood. "Again, I object, Your Honor. There isn't any proof to that statement."

The judge nodded and looked at Hannett. "I'd like to hear your proof for that statement."

"Yes, Your Honor. There were drugs found at the Rawlins residence."

LAUREL WATCHED AS Addy sat up in her bed and talked on the phone. "Yes, Daddy, I've been good for Laurel. Guess what? We went to Mimi and Pops's house for supper. I got to ride on Dandelion, but everybody calls her

Dandi. She's a pony that Pops got for baby Christopher." She giggled. "He's not born, so Pops and Papa Gus said I could ride him. Is that all right?"

The little girl listened. "Yes, Daddy. Laurel walked right by my side and I wore a helmet. She won't let anything happen to me." She listened to her father, then said, "I love you, too. 'Bye." With a big grin, Addy held out the phone. "Daddy wants to talk to you."

Laurel took the phone, anxious to hear what Kase had to say about today. Holding the phone in her hand, Laurel said, "You choose the book you want me to read, and I'll be right back." With the girl's nod, Laurel walked into the hall. "Kase?"

"Hi, Laurel. Damn, it's good to hear your voice."

"It's good to hear yours, too. Rough day?"

"Not the best, but I didn't expect anything less from Ben. He's accusing me of possessing drugs. The only thing that is in my favor is the fact that he entered my house illegally."

Laurel glanced over her shoulder to check on Addy. She lowered her voice to a whisper. "Could the drugs have been Johanna's?"

"More than likely, or maybe Ben planted them."

"My God, would he go that far to get Addy?"

"After today, I'm not putting anything past him."

"Maybe he wants Addy for appearance's sake, or the fact that they weren't the best parents to their daughter?"

"If he wants to be a better grandparent, why would he take a child from her father?" Laurel could hear the pain in his voice. "There's something more he wants, Laurel, and I need to find out what it is before I lose my child. Ben even suggested he and Judith would be better parents to Addy because they have a traditional marriage. That Addy needs the lifestyle that she's been used to."

"You being single shouldn't be an issue. Oh, Kase, I'm so sorry. I wish I could do more."

"You're doing more than you know." He hesitated, then said, "I wish...I was there with Addy...with you."

She swallowed, not wanting to hope. "Pretend I'm sending you a big hug."

"I keep remembering kissing you."

"Kase, you shouldn't be thinking about anything but your daughter."

"You're right. Thank you for being so wonderful with Addy. She needs that now."

Laurel closed her eyes. "You don't have to thank me. She's been a joy." And she was getting too attached to both of them. "Look, Kase. Addy's ready for her story, then I need to get her settled for the night."

"Of course. I'll call tomorrow."

"Goodbye, Kase." Laurel ended the call and sank against the wall. Her heart ached for the man. But she couldn't dream about his kisses, or the way her heart soared when he looked at her. She wasn't a teenager anymore.

If things went bad at the custody hearing, Kase wouldn't have any choice but to move back to Denver to be able to see his daughter.

Laurel's life was here. She had debts to pay and a business to run. If she let herself start dreaming about Kase, she might get hurt again. She had to protect herself, but that wasn't an option anymore. She looked down at the beautiful child surrounded by her dolls in the bed. She smiled. It seemed she'd already fallen in love with both father and daughter.

Chapter Nine

Late the next night, Kase climbed out of his SUV and stretched to get the kinks out. He was weary from the long drive from Denver, but more so from the past two grueling days in front of the judge. Still, nothing had been settled completely.

Worse, he'd been ordered to bring Addy to Denver so she could spend some time with her grandparents. Judge Steffen felt the child had been ripped from their lives so suddenly that he wanted to see some interaction between the three.

Kase hated that his daughter had to go through this, but since Addy's nanny, Mary Beth, would be there to supervise the situation, he didn't fight it, not that it would do him any good. That hadn't stopped his concerns, not only for Addy, but also about the fairness of this case. It was definitely going the Chappells' way. He had to do something to change that.

Right now, he needed sleep. He pulled his suitcase out of the back of his car when he noticed a light in the barn. Had Laurel forgotten to turn it off, or was she out there? He hoped the latter because he needed to see a friendly face. He left his bag in the gravel driveway and walked toward the double doors.

Inside, he heard the soft sound of the radio and the

Garth Brooks song "The Dance." Then he heard a soft, sexy female voice singing along. He walked down the aisle and found Laurel in Honor's stall, brushing her down. The mare loved the attention and the company.

Kase leaned against the post and just enjoyed the view. Laurel's hair was tied back into a loose ponytail, and she was in her standard jeans, boots and a black Henley shirt. She looked so appealing. He wanted nothing more than to touch her, hold her against him, absorbing the feel of her soft body.

There was something about her freshness and innocence that drew him, making him wish he could turn back the clock.

He'd made many mistakes during his years in Denver. Now he hoped to keep Addy from being exposed to that frivolous lifestyle. He didn't want his daughter to be raised like her mother. She needed to learn what was important, to earn her place in life, not have everything handed to her. The most important thing, he wanted her to feel loved. Laurel could teach her those things.

He wanted to feel those things, too.

The woman in question finally looked up from her task, and her eyes widened. "Kase!" She set her brush down, rushed out of the stall and nearly jumped into his arms.

He didn't question her actions but reveled in the pleasure of having her body pressed against him. He inhaled her scent, with a little horse mixed in. The combination was more erotic then he ever could imagine. He released a breath beside her ear and felt her shiver.

Finally she pulled back. "Sorry, I didn't mean to attack you the minute you got here."

He kept his arms around her. He wanted to keep

her close. "I rather enjoyed the way you said 'welcome home.'" He liked it a lot.

Her gaze searched his face. "You look tired. You should go up to the house and get some sleep."

"In a minute. I like where I am right now. You're a breath of fresh air."

She smiled and his heart did a flip. "I wouldn't say that. I've been around horses all day."

"And a four-year-old. How is Addy?"

"She's been wonderful." Laurel's smile grew brighter. "I put her to bed about an hour ago. She said a prayer for you and went right to sleep. But I bet she'd love it if you went in and kissed her good-night."

He caught her hands in his. "How about you, Laurel? Would you like me to kiss you, too? But instead of good-night, how about a hello kiss?"

Laurel's eyes rounded and for a second he thought she might pull away. He was surprised as hell when she gave him a slow nod. "I'd like that."

"Oh, baby, I'd like that, too." He lowered his head and brushed his mouth over hers. She sucked in a breath and he repeated the action, loving her breathy reaction. "I've been thinking about this since I left you early yesterday." His lips caressed hers, gently nibbling, and he was rewarded with her soft moan.

"Oh, Kase…"

That did it. He lowered his head and captured her mouth. He gently ran his tongue over her lips, and when she opened, he slipped inside to taste her.

As the kiss turned bolder, she moved her hands up his chest and looped them around his neck, her body pressed against him, enticing him, testing his will.

He tore his mouth away and kissed her jaw, then he

reached her ear. "Damn, woman," he breathed, feeling her shudder. "What are you doing to me?"

She looked up at him with those incredible green eyes. "Welcoming you home."

With a groan, he went back for another kiss, then another. Suddenly he felt a nudge against his back, then a loud nickering sound. "What the hell?" Kase pulled away and found Honor was behind him.

He couldn't help but laugh as he reached for the bridle and began stroking the horse. "Sorry, girl, were we ignoring you?"

"Oh, Kase, I'm sorry. I should have closed her gate."

"I might have distracted you." Kase petted the mare, and she ate up the attention. "I think she was tired of being ignored."

He walked the horse back to her stall, needing the time to cool down. As much as he wanted Laurel, he knew neither one of them was ready to go the next step. Not until he got Addy's custody issue resolved, and then he'd see if Laurel could forgive him for his past mistakes.

Ten minutes later, the horses settled and the barn quiet, they walked up to the house together. After grabbing his bag, Kase put his other arm around Laurel's shoulders. He wanted her close.

"Do you ever think about…if years ago I hadn't been such a jerk, what would have happened between us?"

"No." She tried to pull away, but he continued toward the back porch.

"Please, talk to me, Laurel," he urged.

Laurel fought the urge to run. She didn't want to spoil their time together. "You've got to be tired, Kase. We can do this another time."

"Most of our time is with Addy. Please, Laurel." He sat down on the porch steps and tugged on her arm, hoping she would join him. "It's been between us since that first day we saw each other in the corral, and I don't want it to be there any longer."

She finally sat down. "I don't know what there is to say, Kase. It's been ten years."

"Okay, I'll say it. I was an arrogant kid who thought he knew everything. I didn't care who I hurt, my dad or you."

She felt tears burning her eyes. "Yeah, you hurt me. I was a teenage girl in love. That last weekend you were home from college, I thought I did something bad, especially since…"

"Since we had sex," he finished for her.

She nodded. She hadn't given in to their passion while they were both in high school. "When you went off to college, I felt you slipping away from me." His hand took hers. "I thought if I gave you what you wanted, it would keep you close to me."

"Then weeks later back at school, I told you I didn't want us to be a couple anymore."

She released a shaky breath and nodded. Why did it still hurt so much? "I was eighteen, and you were my life."

"I'm sorry, Laurel." He squeezed her hand. "Will you let me tell you something?"

The spring evening was cool and she felt a shiver go through her. She stole a glance at him in the night shadows. He wasn't looking at her, but off into the distance.

"I was nineteen, and all I wanted was to leave this small town. The last thing I wanted was to be a rancher. My feelings for you were the one thing that could keep me from my dream."

"But I'd never do that," she insisted. She wanted him to have everything he desired.

"I know, but you still distracted me, and I needed all my focus on college. You'll never know how hard it was to give you up, especially after we made love that day." He cradled her hand in both of his. "It was my first time, too."

She knew that and cherished that memory.

"We kind of fumbled through the learning process together." He sighed as if remembering. "That day meant a lot to me."

"I'm glad," she told him honestly.

"What I want you to know is that I didn't want to break up with you. But after I got back to college, I realized that if I wanted to maintain my grades, I couldn't keep coming home every weekend." His thumb rubbed gently against her palm. "We were both too young to be serious. I thought I did the right thing."

"I know that now," she told him. "And you probably tried to tell me that back then, I just wouldn't listen." She released a long breath. "But that didn't help my hurt."

The long silence was deafening, then Kase said, "Whether you believe me or not, I wanted to call you so many times. I wanted to tell you I made a mistake and beg you to take me back." His gaze met hers. "I missed you so damn much, Laurel."

She would have taken him back in a second. She looked away. "No, you were right, you would have never finished school, let alone law school. You have to be proud of what you accomplished."

Kase shrugged. "Some things, yes. I thought that making a lot of money meant success. By the time I realized I was wrong, I couldn't lose the biggest joy in my life, Addy. Ben's playing hardball, Laurel, and he might take her from me."

Laurel squeezed his hand and leaned her head on his

shoulder. "He won't, Kase. We'll do whatever it takes. You're a good father, and no one will separate you from your daughter." She prayed to God she spoke the truth.

"I love your optimism." He brushed a kiss across her mouth, then stood and tugged at her hand. "Come on, let's go to bed."

She froze, then realized she would love nothing more than to accept his invitation. Together they walked through the quiet house. Gus was in his room downstairs, watching television. Kase stopped by to say goodnight. They talked a few minutes, then he closed the door and came back to her.

They climbed the stairs in silence until they reached the second floor and came to Addy's room. Kase opened the door and was met with a soft glow from the nightlight, illuminating his way to the bed where his daughter slept.

He sat down on the mattress and leaned over to kiss her. "Good night, sweetheart," he whispered as Laurel watched from the doorway.

"Daddy…" The child's sleepy voice was hoarse. "You came home."

"Of course I did. I'd never leave my little girl."

Laurel blinked back tears watching Kase cradle his daughter in his arms. *No, Ben Chappell, you're not separating these two.* Somehow, a judge had to see they belonged together.

Kase stood and came to the door. "'Night, Addy. Go back to sleep and I'll see you in the morning."

He quietly closed the door and turned to Laurel. "Thank you for taking such great care of my daughter."

"There's no thanks needed. Addy is a joy. We had a wonderful time."

He reached for her and wrapped her in his arms. "She

still had to be a handful." He yawned. "I'm sorry, it's just I'm dead on my feet."

"Then go to bed." Suddenly Laurel felt awkward. "Let me just get my things out of your room. I thought I should be close to Addy, so I slept next door. I should head home." She started to walk away, but he pulled her back.

"It's too late to leave, Laurel. I'll sleep in Dad's room." He nodded toward the empty master bedroom. A smile appeared across his face. "I like knowing you were in my bed. Even if I can't be there with you." He leaned down and kissed her long and deep, then when he finally broke it off, she gasped for air. "Good night, Laurel." He turned and walked away.

She sagged against the wall, biting her lip to keep from calling him back. Once she was somewhat recovered from Kase's loving assault, she managed to get to her bedroom and close the door. If she continued to be involved in Kase's life, it wouldn't be long before something happened between them. Was she ready for that? Was she ready to possibly get her heart broken? She thought about Kase's custody hearing, knowing he could leave her and go back to Denver. If he asked her to go with them, would she go, too? That was the big question.

THE NEXT MORNING at the breakfast table, Kase watched Laurel and Addy together. Their interaction made his heart swell. His daughter had come a long way in the past few months, especially since having Laurel in her life. After his confession last night, he wasn't so sure he was worthy of her. *Whoa, don't get ahead of yourself.* He needed to get through this court hearing first, and the request from the judge.

He couldn't hold off any longer. "Addy, I need to talk to you about something."

He glanced at his father, then at Laurel before his attention went back to the tiny four-year-old. "I have to go back to Denver."

Addy's smile disappeared. "No, I want you to stay here. Papa Gus can walk again, and he's going to watch me ride the pony. You promised you would, too."

He hated that he had to do this to her. "And I will, honey, but remember I told you that Grandpa Ben and Grandma Judith miss you." He knew that was a lie. "They want you to come visit them."

Addy's blue eyes rounded. "Are you going to give me back?"

Kase felt his chest tighten. Oh, God. How could she even think that? Kase stood and pulled his daughter into his arms, then sat back down in his chair. "Oh, no, sweetheart. I'm never giving you back." He hugged her small body, his voice rough with emotion. "I love you very much and that will never change. And no one is ever taking you away from me."

"I love you, too, Daddy." She looked up at him as tears filled her eyes. "I don't want to leave you, or Papa Gus, or Laurel."

This was the part that tore at him. "When I go back to Denver at the end of the week, you need to come with me to see your grandparents." He rushed on to say, "Mary Beth will be there, too, so you can spend the night with them." He knew she liked her nanny.

Addy looked thoughtful. "Okay, but I want Laurel to go, too." She turned to Laurel. "Please go with us, Laurel, so I won't be scared."

Laurel's gaze went to Kase. He nodded, praying she'd help out.

"Of course I'll go with you," she said.

Addy looked at her grandpa. "And Papa Gus?"

Gus shook his head. "Can't make this trip, pumpkin. Someone needs to look after the horses." He stood and took hold of his cane. "Now that I can get around, I think I'll head out to the barn. But you three make your plans. It's about time I handle things around here," he mumbled as he grabbed his cowboy hat off the hook and limped out the door.

Laurel spoke up. "Addy, while you're in Denver, maybe your daddy will take you to the zoo or the aquarium. There's a butterfly pavilion, too."

Addy swung around to look at him. "Daddy, I want to go there and pet butterflies."

He smiled. "I don't know if you can pet them, but I'll gladly take you there." He looked at Laurel. He shouldn't, but he wanted to spend time with her, too. "Then it's a date with my girls."

TWO DAYS LATER, barely dawn, Laurel was in her apartment, finishing her packing for the trip to Denver.

Laurel glanced at her mother. "So you think this is a bad idea?"

Diane shrugged. "You're an adult, Laurel. This is your decision. I'm only worried because you're already attached to Addy." She smiled. "That precious little girl has stolen all our hearts."

Laurel continued to put folded clothes in her suitcase. She wasn't even sure what to bring. Outside of her office attire, she didn't own much beyond jeans.

She stopped and looked at her mother. "You haven't said much about Kase."

"I've always liked him, but of course, your father and I were both upset when he hurt you so badly. You were only kids then, but I still don't want to see it happen again."

"So you think I'm being foolish for going to Denver?"

"I'm only saying, you and Kase are both vulnerable right now. He could lose his daughter." Her mother didn't hide her concern. "I can't believe a judge would take her away from her father."

"That's why he needs my support."

Her mother smiled. "I hope he knows how lucky he is to have you."

Laurel zipped up her suitcase and set it on the floor. "Oh, I'm sure if you get the chance, you'll tell him."

"What's a mother for?"

They both laughed, then hugged before Diane started for the door. Outside Laurel saw Chet coming up the stairs. "Hello, Diane, Laurel."

"Hi, Chet," her mother said. "It's nice to see you again. You haven't been up to the house for supper lately."

"Laurel's been keeping me pretty busy. But I'll take an invitation anytime."

"How about Wednesday? Are you free?"

"For your cooking, I'll make sure."

Chet grinned, sending her mother off happy.

"You are such a charmer." Laurel laughed. "I'm surprised you aren't beating the ladies off with a stick."

The good-looking foreman's gaze met hers. "Because someone already has my heart."

Laurel had heard stories but never questioned Chet about his private life. "You need me for something before I leave?"

"Nope, got everything under control." He held out a padded envelope. "This came for you, and I signed for it."

She took the envelope just as Chet's cell phone rang. He looked at the caller ID. "Sorry, I got to take this." He waved and walked off.

Laurel examined the envelope as she walked back

upstairs to the apartment. The return address was a PO box in Denver. She still had no idea who sent it. She tore open the letter and pulled out a bulky folded paper. She gasped as numerous one-hundred-dollar bills fluttered to the floor.

"What in the world?"

She looked at the paper, trying to find an explanation. All that was written was "I hope this helps." That was it? No signature to tell her who sent this money? She quickly gathered up the cash and counted the bills, and the sum startled her. Five thousand dollars!

"Who would send me this kind of money?" she murmured, then suddenly thought of Jack. Was he finally feeling guilty about running off, hoping that this money would stop her father and Trent from prosecuting the theft? She heard her mother's voice from the bottom of the stairs.

"Laurel, Kase just pulled in."

She quickly stuck the money and letter back into the envelope. This wasn't what she needed right now.

Chapter Ten

"Has she finally conked out?" Kase asked, keeping his eyes on the road.

Laurel glanced to the back of the SUV to see Addy sound asleep in her safety seat. "Finally." She faced the front again. "I give her maybe thirty minutes until she's wide-awake again."

"I'll take it." Kase grinned as he drove east along Interstate 70 headed toward Denver. "I'll take any amount for a few minutes of peace and quiet." He reached across the console and took hold of her hand. "So hurry up and let's have some adult conversation. Anything that doesn't involve naming baby dolls, or a discussion about those little yellow characters from her favorite movie."

Laurel swatted at his arm. "Stop it. Addy isn't that bad. And there's nothing wrong with playing with baby dolls."

"Just not 24/7." He glanced at her and smiled. "Now that I have your undivided attention, tell me what's got you so distracted."

He noticed? She thought of the envelope of money hidden in her dresser drawer back at the apartment. Here was her opportunity to tell Kase, but she couldn't. He had too much on his mind without having to deal with her troubles.

"It's nothing," she denied. "I'm just a little tired."

He squeezed her hand. "Are you having second thoughts about coming with us?"

Second, third and fourth doubts.

Before she could answer, he quickly added, "Dammit, Laurel, I didn't want you to feel pressured to come with us."

"I don't," she emphasized. "I wanted to come to help Addy through this." What she wasn't sure about was spending so much alone time with Kase. She could get her heart broken again.

She forced a smile, trying not to think about the sensation he created as his thumb brushed over the back of her hand. "I was actually thinking about Ruby's training. Since the mare's been doing so well, her owner wants me to ride her in the RMRHA Summer Slide."

"The reining futurity, right?"

She nodded. "I'm just not sure it's the right time."

He turned and gave her that familiar sexy grin that had first melted her teenage heart. "I recall you used to kill it when you entered the cutting competitions."

She shrugged. "Reining is a whole different world for me, Kase. I'm not sure if I'm ready."

"You were born ready, Laurel. I've never known anyone who can get a horse to perform like you. If Ruby's owner thinks you're good enough, why not give it a try?"

"There's just been a lot of distractions, and I haven't put in the time I've wanted to."

Kase glanced from the road to her. "That's because we've been taking too much of your time."

"I've loved helping out. But remember I've also been working three mornings a week in the accounting office. I've had to rely a lot on Chet to help with the training, and added to that I haven't competed in a while, and never in the reining arena."

He laced his fingers through hers. "I understand, but I still feel you should seriously think about it. And I'll do whatever I can to help you. How much time before the futurity?"

He was distracting her. "I have until mid-July to decide."

"Then you still have some time. When we get back from this trip, I'll make sure we don't take you away from your training time."

Laurel's chest tightened. Did that mean he was cutting Addy out of her life? "Would I at least get to see Addy occasionally?"

He frowned at her. "You can't think that I meant… Of course, you can. I only meant that I won't have to ask you to pick her up from school, and now that Dad is back on his feet, he can handle our horses." He looked at her again. "How could you think I'd want you out of Addy's life? Or mine?"

She shrugged, not wanting to get excited over his words. "You have a lot to deal with." She looked in the backseat to see the child was still asleep. "You have to think about Addy, Kase. If something happened, you'd have to take her back to Denver…"

"Nothing is going to change, Laurel. The judge is going to award me custody, and Addy is coming home with me."

She felt the tight grip on her hand, knowing that Kase wasn't as confident as he sounded.

TWO HOURS LATER, the bellman escorted them through the double doors of the historic Brown Palace Hotel in downtown Denver. Holding back a gasp, Laurel paused as she looked around the huge atrium-style lobby.

The walls were painted cream and trimmed in a rich honey-colored wainscoting. She tilted her head back to look up at the incredible architecture, the grand archways and golden ornate railings, exposing the numerous floors overhead. In the center of the massive lobby was a sitting area with overstuffed furniture and tables adorned with fresh flowers. Behind it was the sweeping stairs leading up to each floor.

This country girl hadn't seen anything like this, even when she went to visit Brooke and Coralee in Las Vegas this past year. She definitely needed to get off the ranch more often.

She felt a tug on her arm. "Laurel, isn't it pretty?"

She glanced down at the child. "It's very pretty. So are you." They had somehow talked Addy into switching her usual jeans and boots for a pair of pink capris and a butterfly print blouse. Her blond curls were pulled back from her face with bright clips.

"You look pretty, too," Addy said.

"Thank you, sweetie."

Laurel had chosen a pair of black slacks and a cream-colored silk blouse. Looking around at the five-star hotel's clientele, and even though there were plenty of cowboy types, she was glad she'd ditched her usual jeans.

She glanced at Kase. He had on dark slacks and a dress shirt and loafers. This was Kase's world, and she couldn't help but wonder if she would fit in. She put on a smile as he approached them and Addy ran into his arms. She wanted to follow the child. She wanted to pretend they were a family.

"It's beautiful."

Addy smiled. "It's so pretty, Daddy. Maybe a princess lives here."

He winked at her. "You and Laurel are the only princesses here now."

He leaned toward Laurel's ear. "I chose this place hoping you'd like it."

"Thank you," she told him, just as a handsome man in his midthirties wearing a slate-gray business suit walked up to them.

"Mr. Rawlins, it's good to have you back with us."

"Thank you, Kyle. It's nice to be back. This is my daughter, Addy, and my friend Laurel Quinn. Laurel and Addy, this is Kyle Hutchins. If there is anything you need, he'll find it for you."

"I'll do my best." Kyle smiled. "It's my pleasure, Miss Quinn and Miss Addy, to have you at our hotel."

The child giggled. And Laurel said, "Thank you, Kyle. Like I was telling Kase, you have a beautiful hotel."

"I'm glad you like it. We've tried to keep its centuries-old charm, along with some modern conveniences." He turned to Kase. "We have your suite ready, and I also made a lunch reservation for you at the hotel restaurant, or I can have lunch sent up to your suite."

Addy's head resting on her daddy's shoulder signaled to Laurel the child needed a nap. "Daddy, I want some mac and cheese."

"Sounds good, sweetie." Kase shifted Addy in his arms. "Maybe upstairs might be best."

Laurel nodded in agreement and the concierge escorted them to the bank of elevators. Addy had to press the button, and the doors opened with a chime. Kase let Laurel in ahead of him and followed with Addy. Once on the ninth floor, Kyle led them down the hall of the historic hotel, then opened the door to their suite.

Laurel's heart began to race as she stepped into the large sitting area. The oversize furniture was elegant and comfortable looking. The dark hues of the leather sofa, and the contrast of the light gray walls, showed off the richness of the wood. A row of windows exposed the Denver skyline.

Doubts filled her head once again. She couldn't help but wonder if coming here was the right thing to do. She was a small-town girl who raised and trained horses. She'd been to the state capital before, but never experienced this side of the city.

Kyle motioned with his left hand. "I'll put your daughter's suitcase in the smaller bedroom, and you and Miss Quinn in the bigger room."

Laurel's eyes grew wide. Oh, dear Lord, was she ready for this?

Quickly, Kase set him straight. "Miss Quinn and my daughter will be staying together. Give them the bigger room, please."

Kyle didn't blink. He walked away and gave instructions to the bellboy.

Soon the task was completed, and there was a knock on the door. Addy's dish of macaroni and cheese had arrived, along with two club sandwiches and green salads. They sat down and ate an early lunch, then Kase convinced Addy to take a nap before they headed for the aquarium. Although the four-year-old argued, she'd barely finished her food before she crashed on her bed.

TWENTY MINUTES LATER, Kase saw Laurel quietly tiptoe from the large master bedroom so as not to disturb the child, but the minute she closed the bedroom door she turned and found Kase. He walked up to her and cupped her face. "I've been wanting to do this since I picked you up this morning." He lowered his head and captured her mouth.

Kase shifted his stance and drew Laurel against his body, and kissed her as if he were a starving man. He pressed closer, letting her feel what she did to him whenever she was near. He held her tight, relishing the fact she was here. She had no idea how much he needed her, not just physically, but her strength and support.

He broke off the kiss, and his gaze locked on hers. "Have I told you how glad I am that you came with me?"

"I think you just did." She smiled. "And I like that you're glad."

He kissed her once more, then took her hand and walked into the sitting area, and they sat on the tufted leather sofa. He wanted to tell her so many things. He kissed her fingertips.

"Laurel, I've made so many mistakes over the years, but the biggest one was leaving you."

She turned to him and placed her finger over his mouth. "Kase, don't go there. You can never regret going after your dream of becoming a lawyer, or being a father to your wonderful daughter. Addy is such a blessing."

"I know that, and she's so precious to me, and Dad, too. All those years we lost touch…" His eyes met hers. "Six months ago when I called and asked to come home, Dad welcomed Addy and me with open arms."

She turned to face him. "That's what parents do, Kase. My mom and dad have never said, 'I told you so.' They were just there to support me, even when I made mistakes."

They both knew she was talking about Jack. The last thing he wanted was to bring up any ex-boyfriends. But he knew it was between them. Kase reached out and touched her cheek. "I'm so sorry that you had to go through that. If I ever see the guy…"

"No, don't, Kase. Jack's not worth it."

"You must have thought he was."

She glanced away, but not before he saw her sadness. "Laurel, what aren't you telling me?"

She finally looked at him. "I knew what I was getting into with Jack."

No way she could have known. "You knew he was a thief?"

She shook her head. "No, but I knew from Trent's PI report he had a gambling problem."

He didn't understand any of this. "Then why did you want to marry him?"

"Sometimes being alone is worse. Do you remember the population of Hidden Springs? There are nine thousand one hundred and eighty-two men, women and children. I was everyone's kid sister." Her eyes were watery with tears. "Even my twin sister, Brooke, comes here and finds love. Jack said the right words and showed me attention."

His heart was breaking into a thousand pieces. He reached out and stroked her hair. "Do you know how special you are?"

She shrugged. "My parents tell me all the time."

"Well, let me tell you something, too. I don't think of you like a sister. I think of you as a woman. A woman I desire very much." He touched her face. "I want you, Laurel. We may have some obstacles in our way, but that's not going to stop me." He brushed his mouth over hers and loved hearing her intake of breath. "I wish I could offer you more, but right now…"

She placed her lips against his. When she finally broke off the kiss, she said, "No promises, Kase. That way no one has any expectations. I'm here for you and Addy. So it's all good for now."

He wanted more. Not the girl he once knew, but the beautiful, giving woman she'd turned into. Would she give him a second chance? His thoughts turned to his daughter. Would he get that second chance to be a father? He cradled Laurel's head against his chest. How he prayed he didn't let either one of them down.

"Look at all the pretty fishes, Daddy," Addy announced as they walked through the tunnel-like glass enclosure at the Downtown Aquarium. Sea life was all around them. "Laurel, look!"

"I see them."

Laurel smiled, trying to push aside her fatigue. After getting up at dawn, they'd spent the past few hours walking through several of the aquarium's exhibits, the underwater sea, the rain forest, the coral lagoon and Addy's favorite, the Mystic Mermaids show.

She was happy that the four-year-old had taken her attention off Kase. But nothing could erase the memory of his kisses, his touch and his mouth moving over her skin. Although they hadn't made love, Kase let her know how much he desired her. And he practically had her begging for more. She was getting in deep, but she didn't want to stop.

First and foremost, she had to remember they were here to help Addy, and make sure she could handle going with her grandparents tomorrow.

She stole another glance at Kase. Standing there holding his daughter in his arms, he pointed out the different fish to the youngster. He tipped his head back and laughed at something Addy said and something shifted in Laurel's chest. Suddenly *sexy* took on an entirely different picture with this father-and-daughter combo.

"Laurel, Laurel, that fish is yellow and black."

Laurel stepped up to the enclosure. "I like that blue one."

"So many pretty colors." The child giggled with excitement. "I feel like I'm swimming with them."

"How about if we eat with them?" Kase announced.

"Daddy, I can't go in the water."

"Well, there's a restaurant that we can go to." He took Laurel's hand. "Come on, I'm getting hungry."

As they walked together, Kase silently thanked Kyle for putting this excursion together on short notice. As a father, he wanted to make the trip special for Addy, help relax her before she headed off with the Chappells tomorrow. He squeezed Laurel's hand. She'd been the one who helped the most, and Addy relied on her, too. He found that he didn't want to be without her, either. Maybe he could find a way to convince her to take a chance on him again.

It was a short distance to the restaurant, and the hostess seated them close to the wall-to-wall fish tank. The waitress brought a special children's menu for Addy, and the child loved the attention from everyone.

The young waitress named Lisa looked at Laurel. "Your daughter looks just like you."

Kase watched Laurel's surprised reaction.

Blushing, she smiled. "Thank you."

Lisa handed them the menus and walked off.

The conversation didn't get past Addy. "She said you were my mom." The child's blue eyes widened, then just as quickly the joy faded. "I wish you were."

Chapter Eleven

By nine o'clock, Kase had said good-night to his daughter and left the master bedroom. Laurel remained, promising Addy she'd stay until she fell asleep. Besides, she wasn't ready to be alone with Kase.

Call her chicken, but she wasn't ready to deal with her feelings for the man. There was too much going on. She couldn't help but think about the mess in her life. There was the money hidden back in her apartment, and she was pretty sure it came from Jack. What if he'd gotten it illegally? If she was connected to something bad, could that jeopardize Addy's custody? God, she prayed not.

She heard her phone chime. She'd turned off the ringer earlier so as not to disturb Addy.

She slowly rolled over to see a message from Kase.

She pressed the button to read, R U hiding from me? K.

She typed back, Just tired. Long day.

Need to talk about court. No little ears.

She sighed. OK B out.

She got off the bed and gathered her hair into a pony-tail. *Be strong, and don't do anything stupid like let him kiss you.*

After one more look at the sleeping Addy, she silently opened the door and walked out to the sitting room.

She paused as she saw Kase standing at the window looking out at the city lights. He was in his socks, his shirt pulled from his jeans.

Drawn by the beautiful scene, she walked across the plush carpet to join him. She was surprised to see a long-neck bottle of the local-brewed beer. He held it up. "Join me?"

She had an automatic denial ready, then she saw something in his eyes and quickly changed her mind. "Sure."

She watched him go to the minibar and take out another bottle. After using the opener, he walked back to her in a long, easy gait that reminded her of the teenage Kase she'd once known and loved. *Oh, no. Don't go thinking about your past together.*

"Thank you." She accepted the beer, took a drink and turned toward the window.

After enjoying the view a few minutes, Kase finally spoke. "My lawyer called me. Ben and Judith will be in the lobby tomorrow at nine o'clock to pick up Addy."

Laurel sighed, wishing she had some encouraging words to give him. "They'll only have her twenty-four hours, Kase. And her nanny will be there, too. You said Addy loves Mary Beth."

He looked down at his beer. "I know. I just wish I didn't have to put her through this. Not with everything else that's happened to her." He cursed. "Dammit, Laurel. Why are they doing this? Neither one of them wants this child. I know that in my gut. There has to be another reason."

Hearing the anguish in his voice, she wrapped her arms about him. "It's going to be all right, Kase," she promised. "The judge can't take her away without a reason."

He held her tight, as if she were his lifeline. "I pray you're right, Laurel. I don't know what I'd do if I lost her."

He held her for a long time, then finally looked down at her. "Have I told you how happy I am that you're here with us?"

She smiled. "Yes, you have. But, really, Kase, it's my pleasure."

"No, it's mine." He took their bottles and set them on the glass-top table, then cupped her cheeks, and his mouth captured hers in a tender kiss that quickly became all-consuming. So much for her resolve. She wrapped her arms about his neck and pressed her body against his.

He tore his mouth away, his eyes searching hers. "I need you here, Laurel," he breathed. "I don't think I've ever stopped needing you."

She wanted to confess her feelings right back at him, but something stopped her—panic, fear, maybe the uncertainty of their future. She needed to protect her heart. How could she when he'd already stolen it? She said good-night and turned and walked back to her room. Alone.

THE NEXT MORNING, both Kase and Laurel put on a big, bright smile for Addy as they rode the elevator down to the lobby. Of course, the little girl was wise to their attempt.

"It's okay, Daddy. I won't cry, but can I miss you?"

Kase nearly broke down as he pulled her into a tight hug. "Oh, sweetie," he breathed against her ear, nearly choking on his emotions. "Yes, because I'm gonna miss you, too."

Suddenly the double doors opened just as Laurel hugged Addy goodbye.

Ben Chappell demanded attention, even if it wasn't deserved. About six feet tall, he kept himself trim. The sixty-year-old lawyer had built his prestigious law firm with hard work and by marrying a wealthy philanthropist's daughter, Judith Kirsch.

Ben crossed the lobby, dressed in a pair of tan chinos and a navy polo shirt. "Kase, where's my granddaughter?"

Laurel walked Addy over to them. "She's here." Kase leaned forward and in a low voice said, "You hurt her and you answer to me."

"Is that a threat?"

"Of course not, but it's a damn harsh warning. I'll see you in court at nine o'clock tomorrow."

Kase bent down and kissed his daughter's cheek just as Mary Beth came through the hotel doors. The fifty-something woman was a retired teacher, and since her husband's death, she had worked as a nanny.

"Mary Beth," Addy cried and ran off toward her.

Mary Beth waved to Kase, then took Addy's hand and walked out the door. Kase's chest constricted painfully and he fought to keep from running after his child.

He felt Laurel's hand on his arm. "Come on, we're going to get out of here," she said.

He didn't want to go anywhere but to the bar to get good and drunk. "Where are you taking me?"

"First, we're going to have some breakfast. And before you argue, you didn't eat anything this morning."

"I don't have much of an appetite."

"Well, change your mind, because we're going to do some walking today. Kyle told me there's a historical city tour. You know, from back in the gold rush days."

He frowned. "Really, that interests you?"

"Well, since they don't have horses readily available, walking is the next best thing to get rid of stress. Come on, it will do us both some good."

He tried not to smile, but too late—she saw it. He pulled her into his arms. "Probably would be good, but I know something else that would distract me."

She blushed and he loved it. "Sorry, that's not on the day's schedule." Although she didn't pull away. "And I believe you need to speak to your real estate agent this afternoon."

He didn't want to deal with business now, but he had no choice. He wanted to get rid of the house and all the memories from the past. Until then, he couldn't think about a future for him and Addy. One that he hoped included Laurel.

"Okay, let's get started." He glanced down at her cream-colored, cable-knit sweater, white capri pants and deck shoes. "So where do you want to eat?"

She beamed. "There's a café not far from here."

"Okay, I'm in your hands, so lead the way."

She gave him a smile that melted his heart, and he followed her out the door. Ah, hell, he'd follow her anywhere.

AT FOUR O'CLOCK that afternoon, Kase drove the twenty-minute trip from Denver to Aurora, Colorado. When he pulled the SUV into the long stone-pavered driveway and parked in front of the massive home, Laurel's mouth dropped open. This wasn't a house, this was a mansion.

She looked at the stone-and-stucco, two-story home, similar to a Craftsman-style, but on a huge scale. He helped her out of the car, but she wasn't sure if she wanted to go inside. This had been where Kase lived with his wife for the past five years. Laurel could almost understand why he'd left her behind. She wouldn't fit in here.

"Johanna was the one who picked out this house. I just went along with her choice."

She stared at the twelve-foot-high dark wood doors and released a breath. "It's a little overpowering. I can understand why Addy was scared."

"I don't want to live here, either, not back then and not today especially. That's why I'm selling this place, and moving on with Addy. Our lives are back in Hidden Springs."

She wanted to believe him, but her doubt lingered. After this lavish lifestyle, could Kase be happy on the small ranch?

"If you'd rather go back to the hotel, I'll reschedule with the Realtor…"

"No, I'm curious. It's lovely."

He slipped his hand over hers and together they walked up to the house. He took out a key, unlocked the door and swung it open. She went in first, and he followed behind. After dealing with the security system, he returned to her. She looked down at the planked hardwood floors of the massive entry that led to a sweeping open staircase. Off to her left, there was a sunken living room with a floor-to-ceiling limestone fireplace.

"Wow. You could get lost in here."

Even though there was furniture in all the rooms, the place echoed not just with their voices, but also with emptiness. This wasn't a home. It was a showplace.

He nodded. "I know. When I came home from work, I usually stayed in the back of the house." He took her hand and tugged her past the staircase to an open kitchen and family room with another fireplace. Besides a bathroom, there was a den with a large desk.

"I worked in here."

His gaze locked on hers, as if waiting for some sort of reaction. "If you like, I'll take you upstairs to look around."

She shook her head. "I think I've seen all I need to see." She went into the kitchen and ran a hand over the smooth marble countertops. "My mother would love this room." A huge side-by-side refrigerator glistened in the sunlight coming through the French doors.

"The place is like new. Johanna never cooked, not for me anyway. Mary Beth fixed meals for Addy."

"It seems like such a shame to let all this space go to waste."

He went to her and pulled her into his arms. "It took me a lot of years, Laurel, but I realize now what I thought I wanted wasn't all this." His gaze moved to hers, and the silver depths held her attention. "Sometimes it takes a long time to realize that everything I really wanted was right in front of me all along."

AT EIGHT O'CLOCK that evening, Laurel stood in front of the mirror in her bedroom, eyeing the simple black skirt that hit her just below the knees. A sleeveless rose-colored silk shirt draped over her breasts and was cinched at the waist with a silver belt. She slipped on a sheer off-white sweater. She wore her hair down and her ears were adorned with silver hoops.

Satisfied with the results, she stepped into a pair of black sandals and grabbed her purse off the bed. After she released a nervous breath, she headed into the sitting room to once again find Kase standing at the window, the Denver skyline glistening as a backdrop.

He wore slate-gray slacks and a black linen shirt. She liked this look on him as much as him in jeans and boots.

He turned around and his gaze slowly moved over her, from the top of her head down to her painted toes.

She had trouble breathing.

"You look amazing." He walked over and kissed her, slow and tender but with enough sizzle to get her humming. He broke off the kiss. "You have no idea how much I want to keep you right here."

She found she'd been thinking about the same thing since this trip began. "If you'd rather not, we don't have to go out."

He groaned. "Oh, yes, we do. At the least, we both need to eat." He took her hand and they headed out the door.

They rode the elevator down and crossed the lobby to the Palace Arms Restaurant. The hostess met them at the entrance. "We've been expecting you, Mr. Rawlins and Miss Quinn."

The young girl escorted them through the restaurant to a corner table. Kase pulled out Laurel's chair, then sat next to her.

She had trouble holding back her excitement. She hadn't been on a date in a while, and she'd never been taken to places like this. Even with Jack, they usually hung out in her apartment, or had gone to a movie. So this was how grown-ups did things?

"Oh, Kase, this is a lovely place."

"I hope you like the food here."

Two glasses of water were delivered along with menus. Once the waiter left, she said, "Kase, you don't need to impress me with extravagant hotels and restaurants. I enjoy just being with you. Of course, your sweet little girl is a nice bonus."

He paused, leaning closer. She could see that silver

glint in his eyes. "So it's not me, it's my child who has you so attentive."

She laughed, not wanting to rattle off all his attributes. She sobered, feeling his heat, inhaling his woodsy scent and loving that he was so close. "Maybe I'll tell you later."

He gave her a slow, sexy smile and she found she was about to give him anything he wanted, her body and soul. She'd never felt this way before.

"Let's see if I can change your mind."

Kase ordered a bottle of wine as Laurel looked around the room. There were several couples dining. Young and old, they seemed comfortable in their surroundings, enjoying each other's company.

She sighed and looked at Kase. Suddenly, doubts hit her, and she felt tongue-tied over what to talk about. What did he expect from her? This night was for them, without Addy between them.

The waiter poured the white wine into Kase's glass. He sampled it, then nodded his approval. Once her glass was filled, Laurel took a quick sip.

She glanced up and saw Kase's gaze on her. "Is there something on my face?" she asked.

He shook his head. "I'm sorry, I didn't mean to make you feel uncomfortable. I just love looking at you."

She took another drink, hoping the alcohol would take effect. "I like looking at you, too," she admitted.

He smiled and took her hand. Bringing it to his lips, he kissed her fingertips. "I'm glad."

She enjoyed the warmth of his hand. "Thank you for bringing me here, Kase. The hotel and restaurant are… lovely, amazingly beautiful. I just can't think of enough adjectives to describe all this."

"I'm glad you like it here. I wanted this time to be

good for all of us. And I'm not going to mention my daughter's name because this evening is just for us."

Laurel couldn't help but smile. "I agree, but I'll say one thing about she-who-shall-not-be-named, she was a hoot yesterday at the aquarium. And I loved sharing it with her. Thank you for bringing me along."

"What about me? Do you like being with me, too?"

His eyes were a bright silver hue, and she felt a little tongue-tied. She blamed it on the wine. "Of course I enjoyed being with you." She knew she was admitting a lot, but she didn't care.

"And I loved being with both of my girls."

He leaned forward, just inches from her face. "Your mouth is sexy. If we were alone, I would be kissing you by now."

Laurel took another drink of wine to help her dry throat. If this was a dream, she wanted it to keep going, and never wake up.

"Yours isn't so bad, either."

He grinned, and her heart went speeding off. Could he hear it pounding?

"We should probably eat something. Wine on an empty stomach isn't wise." He motioned for the waiter. Immediately the young man appeared and they both ordered green salads, and for the main course, beef Wellington.

A breadbasket suddenly arrived on the table. Laurel began to nibble away while listening to Kase's plans for the ranch.

"Dad is a proud man, so any of the changes and repairs, I have to do slowly while trying to convince him they're needed. I've repaired several stalls in the horse barn, but what I'd like to do is build another barn, and buy more quality breeding stock."

She giggled. "Well, if you get the mares, I have the stud."

Kase's gut tightened as he watched Laurel smile. She was so beautiful. He knew she was nervous the moment they sat down. This had to be awkward for her, but she fit in perfectly for him.

He shook his head. "I think I'll wait until I see what that wild stallion of yours has produced before we do a repeat."

"You know, I really tried to stop Wind that day," she said.

"And that would have been reckless," he said. "You know better than to get in the middle of breeding animals. You could have been trampled."

She shook her head. "Wind would never hurt me."

"That day, your stallion had one thing on his mind."

She smiled innocently at him. "Don't most males?"

He started to argue, but he had nothing, especially if she knew what he was thinking right now.

TWO HOURS LATER, full from dinner, they walked a few blocks to a small piano bar where a female singer, Caitlin, performed everything from old forties songs to classic country.

The room was dimly lit and filled with couples more interested in each other than the entertainment.

Kase looked at Laurel across the cozy booth. She was drinking ginger ale with lime, and he had a beer. He'd suggested coming here because he didn't want their evening to end.

"Enjoying yourself?" he asked.

She smiled. "Yes, very much. She has such a pretty voice."

He leaned close and spoke in her ear. "I'm enjoying just being with you…"

She looked at him, her eyes dark with desire. The music started and Caitlin began a Celine Dion song, "Have You Ever Been in Love."

Kase placed his arm around Laurel's shoulders and pulled her against him. "I like to feel you close, Laurel." He kissed her gently, tenderly, as the singer crooned words he wished he had the right to say.

He felt Laurel shiver and his body stirred to life. "I want you, Laurel, more than I've ever wanted anyone… ever."

He watched her swallow hard. "I want you, too, Kase."

It was his turn to swallow, his throat suddenly dry. "I want to take you back to the hotel…if you're ready."

She touched his face. "I've been ready for a long time."

Chapter Twelve

Around eleven o'clock, Kase took Laurel by the hand as they walked through the hotel doors and silently crossed the lobby to the elevators. The place was quiet, but the staff still greeted them. Those had been the only words spoken so as not to break the spell as they rode upstairs to their suite.

Alone in the elevator, Kase fought to keep from grabbing hold of Laurel. He managed to corral his hunger and escorted her down the hall. Once he opened the suite door, Laurel walked in ahead of him. He suddenly couldn't wait any longer and reached for her. He hesitated only to see if she wanted him to go on. "I'm leaving this up to you, Laurel. If you've changed your mind, just walk into your room. I won't push you into anything."

She raised up on her toes and placed a soft kiss on his lips, then met him eye to eye. "I want you, Kase." Her voice was laced with need. "I've always wanted you."

She pulled his mouth back down to hers. This time the kiss was more demanding, driving his own hunger.

"You got me." He scooped her into his arms and carried her into his room. Once he set her down beside the bed, he bent and captured her mouth again and again. Although it nearly killed him, he wanted to savor this time, tasting, then delving into a deep kiss that drugged his senses.

A slow heat began burning through his body and he couldn't find a way to stop it. His lips traveled down the curve of her neck, feeling the throbbing pulse.

"I think we have too many clothes on." He tugged her sweater off her and tossed it on the chair. Next came her top. He tugged the fabric from the waistband of her skirt and up over her head, leaving her in a sheer lace bra.

He swallowed back the dryness. "Oh, Lord, you're beautiful."

"Not what you expected a cowgirl to wear?"

"It's a nice surprise."

"I like surprises, too." Laurel stepped in and began to unbutton his shirt, then removed it, and her hands were on his chest, next her mouth.

He groaned and closed his eyes as she placed soft kisses along his skin. He shivered and managed to tolerate the exquisite agony. He finally put a stop to it. "My turn."

Capturing her wrists firmly in one hand, he trailed his finger along her lips, continuing down her throat, raising goose bumps along the way as he unhooked her bra in the front, then continued the journey, gliding his fingers over her exposed flesh.

"Beautiful…" he breathed, then leaned down and captured her puckered nipple in his mouth.

Laurel was unraveling as she held Kase's head to her breasts. Slow, silky moans escaped her throat. She loved his hands on her and was quickly becoming frantic with need.

Her heart pounding in her ears, she broke his hold and unfastened her skirt, allowing it to drop to the floor. That left her in only her panties and sandals and a lot of goose bumps. She locked on his gaze, his eyes smoky with desire.

He reached for his belt and removed it, kicked off his shoes, then came his trousers. Once he was in his boxers, he pulled the covers back, then he laid her down on the cool sheet.

She cupped his face. "Make love to me, Kase."

"Oh, baby, I plan to."

"Please, hurry." She raised her body against his and he released a groan, then began to trail kisses down her body, paying special attention to her breasts.

Kase raised his head, then lifted his body over hers and paused. "Look at me, Laurel," he said in a husky voice. "I want to see your face."

Laurel obeyed, and a soft groan escaped her lips as she felt her body arch toward his. She breathed his name and they became one…and he took her to heaven.

KASE BLINKED AT the emotion that caught him off guard. He was speechless as to what had just happened between them. He tucked her close to his side, not ready to let her go.

"Are you all right?" he finally asked her.

He felt her smile against his chest and she nodded. "Better than," she told him.

"Better than what?"

She braced her hands on his chest and lifted her head. "Oh, maybe Christmas morning, my mother's apple pie, best day of training, a new foal being born."

He couldn't help but laugh. "Okay, so maybe I needed my ego stroked a little."

In the dim light, he watched as she turned serious. "I've never made love like that, Kase. Ever. No other man has made me feel like you do. How is that?"

He pulled her up to his body and kissed her. He'd never been this happy, and if only things were resolved with Addy, this weekend might have a different outcome. Right now, he had to remain silent with any promises.

Laurel turned serious. "Now I'm going to ask you. Are you all right?"

"How can I not be?" He locked his gaze on her. "I just made love to a beautiful woman I care for very much."

He held her close, enjoying the aftermath of their loving. It didn't take long for the outside world to intrude, and his thoughts turned to his daughter.

Laurel raised her head. "It's hard not to think about her."

He started to speak, but she stopped him. "It's okay, really. I'm thinking about Addy, too." She pressed a kiss against his lips. "That little girl means a lot to me, too. And whatever the judge comes back with tomorrow, I'll be there with you and Addy. I'll do anything to help you keep that little girl. She needs her daddy in her life."

His heart bursting, Kase rolled over and placed Laurel under him. He brushed away strands of hair from her face. He kissed the corner of her mouth, then the middle and the other side. "You're incredible, Laurel. I have many regrets in my life, and you are the biggest one. I should have never pushed you away."

She placed a finger over his mouth. "No regrets tonight. There's just you and me. And we're together right now. That's all that matters."

The moment took on a feeling that left him lighter, freer than he'd felt in a long time. Maybe they all would be given a second chance.

He leaned down and kissed her, and stroked her body to life, hoping he could show her how much he cared. He was in too deep to back away now. Never again would he leave this woman.

THE NEXT MORNING, they woke early and concentrated on getting ready for court. The one good thing about not being able to sleep, he wasn't alone. He had Laurel beside him, eager to distract him with her own special loving.

They got breakfast from room service, then took a cab to the courthouse by eight forty-five to find his lawyer already there. They were back in the judge's chambers. Laurel was going to stay out in the hall, but Kase refused to let her go and talked her into coming inside with them.

Laurel reluctantly agreed but couldn't stop her racing heart. She sat in the back in a chair by the door while Kase went off with his lawyer toward the desk.

When the doors opened again, Ben and Judith Chappell walked in, behind them Mary Beth and Addy. Laurel's heart soared at seeing the child. Immediately the little girl broke away from the nanny and went into her arms. "Laurel! Laurel!" she cried as she hugged her. "I missed you."

"I missed you, too, Addy." She relished in the feel of having the sweet child close. She kissed her head, then said, "I think your daddy wants to see you, too."

Addy grinned and the child took off toward Kase. "Daddy!"

Kase caught her in a flying leap. Laurel's throat tightened at seeing the two together. She glanced back to the Chappells and noticed they didn't look happy at the scene.

Judge Steffen came in from the front and everyone stood. Once he seated himself behind the desk, he looked at the Chappells. "I take it you had the child overnight?"

Ben nodded. "Yes, Your Honor. We had a lovely time. We went out to dinner and Addy played in her old bedroom with some of her toys."

The judge looked at Addy and smiled. "Hello, Addy.

My name is Judge Steffen and I was wondering if we could talk."

At first Addy buried her face in her daddy's shirt. After a few words from Kase, she sat up and nodded.

With the judge's instruction, Mary Beth took the child's hand and walked her up to him. She helped Addy into a seat, then sat down not far from her.

Laurel was relieved that the girl would have someone to go to if she felt panicked.

The judge leaned closer. "Addy, can you tell me how old you are?"

She held up four fingers. "I'm four years old and I go to Saint Theresa Preschool."

The judge smiled. "Such a big girl."

"I am. I don't take naps anymore." With a glare at her grandfather, she sent a clear message.

"Do you have friends at your school?"

She nodded. "Yes, Kelly is my best friend. And sometimes when Chelsea is nice, I play with her, too. But some days she's mean and I have to tell my teacher, Miss Julie."

"How about at home? Do you like living on a ranch?"

She nodded. "Yes. I'm a cowgirl now. I have boots and a hat I wear when I ride a pony."

Judith sucked in an audible breath.

Addy hurried to say, "It's okay, Grandma Judy. Laurel walks with me and I have to wear a helmet so I won't get hurt." She looked up at the judge. "Laurel is the best rider and is the best trainer in the whole world." Addy turned to Laurel and smiled.

The Chappells' lawyer stood. "I object, Your Honor. It's clear the child has been coached with her answers."

"Counselor, let me stress again, this is an informal hearing, and a delicate situation." He nodded toward the child. "So please refrain from any more outbursts."

Addy agreed with the judge and said, "And you didn't raise your hand. That's rude. That means not nice or polite. That's what Miss Julie taught me at my school."

Laurel wanted to stand and cheer. *Way to go, Addy. You tell them.*

The judge turned back to the child. "Addy, did you enjoy being with your grandparents?"

"They are nice, but I want to go home with my daddy and Papa Gus."

The judge continued on. "Wouldn't it be nice to have a woman living with you?"

Those blond curls bobbed as the child nodded. "I have Laurel. She's with me and takes care of me sometimes. So does Papa Gus, but he had to get his hip fixed and he couldn't walk. So when Daddy had to come here before, Laurel stayed at the house."

Judith didn't stay quiet this time. "It's barely been a year, and already Kase has removed our daughter from Addy's life. That's not right."

"No, Grandma Judy, my mom didn't want me." Big tears filled the child's eyes. "Laurel loves me. So I want her to be my mom."

Addy scooted down from the chair and hurried to get to Laurel and climbed into her lap.

The judge looked at her. "Well, Miss Quinn, it seems this child is under the impression that you and her father are going to be a family. Is that true?"

Laurel swallowed and looked at Kase. He smiled and nodded. She'd said she'd do anything, and she didn't hesitate. "Yes, Kase and I have discussed being a family." She just hadn't said the conversation had been ten years ago.

THE COURT DIDN'T adjourn for another hour. After Addy's testimony, the judge had Mary Beth take the child from the room. Kase had tried to assure his daughter that he'd be out soon. He was grateful that Laurel followed them out, too.

Once the door closed, the fireworks began. The Chappells' lawyer went after Kase, accusing him of knowing of Johanna's drug problem and doing nothing to help her. When they hadn't offered any proof of that accusation, Judith went on to testify that her daughter had been left alone for long periods of time. Kase had never been home, not for his wife or child. Then the woman tossed in that Kase had married Johanna only for her money and name.

Kase accounted for every hour he'd worked, and documented the day he'd moved out of the house and began his legal separation from Johanna. He was glad that Laurel wasn't hearing about his failings as a husband and a father.

The worst, the judge hadn't rendered a decision. He told Kase to take his daughter home and he'd be in contact with his decision. Not what Kase wanted to hear. Of course, why was there even a custody hearing?

The Chappells left the courtroom without so much as a goodbye to Addy. Kase took his daughter and Laurel back to the hotel to pack, and within an hour, they were headed back to Hidden Springs. Not the happy ending Kase wanted, but at least he still had his daughter.

With Addy nearly asleep in the backseat, he had time to wonder about the answer Laurel gave the judge. Had she been thinking about them being a family for real, or was it just for the judge? Either way, he couldn't even think about a future, and according to the Chappells, he wasn't good husband or father material. With his past, maybe they were right.

Exhausted, Laurel worked to find a more comfortable

position in the car, wishing she could just go to sleep like Addy. No way would her mind stop replaying what had happened in the courtroom.

Had she hurt or helped Kase and Addy's case? She'd never forgive herself if she'd made matters worse. She remembered the glare that Judith Chappell sent her before she walked out. She understood she lost her daughter, and Addy was her granddaughter, but Laurel would do anything to help Kase keep his child.

She reached over the console and touched his hand. "It's going to be okay, Kase. There's nothing to keep the judge from ruling in your favor."

"You weren't there to hear the Chappells' accusations." He blew out a tired breath. "I have this feeling they're going to try to dig up something else to incriminate me."

"Don't think about anything but the fact you're taking Addy home today. It's going to be fine, Kase, I know it." She prayed that was true.

He finally smiled. "You're right. We had a great weekend together with Addy."

She smiled back at him. No matter what happened she'd never forget last night. "I had a wonderful time, and so did Addy."

"I'm glad, because us being together meant a lot to me. You're so special to me, Laurel. It's just that I managed to destroy my marriage and career." He glanced across the car. "Maybe you should think twice about getting mixed up with a guy like me. Again."

Was he trying to end it? Her heart sank. "Stop, Kase. A marriage takes two people to keep it together. As for your career, you gave that up to be a father to Addy. As for us, we already decided not to make any promises to each other. Not until Addy's case is over."

He nodded. "You're right."

Laurel already knew his daughter had to come first. And if the unthinkable happened, and he lost Addy, Kase would definitely move back to Denver. He'd make his life there so he could be close to his child. That was one of the reasons she loved him so much. She might just have to give him up...again.

LATER THAT EVENING, back in her apartment, Laurel was tired from the trip, but sleep eluded her. She missed being with Kase and Addy. They'd been like a family the past few days, but now she was back to reality. And alone.

Suddenly she heard a soft knock on her door. Dressed in a long T-shirt, she slipped on a robe, wondering if there was a problem with one of the horses. To her surprise, when she looked out the peephole, she found Kase standing on her stoop.

She pulled open the door. "Kase! What's the matter? Is it Addy?"

He stepped inside and took her into his arms. "No, it's me. I missed you." His mouth found hers, hungry and demanding. By the time he released her, they were both breathless.

"Sorry, I shouldn't come after you that way. It's just that..."

She'd never seen him so distraught. "Kase, talk to me."

He paced, then stopped to look at her. "God, Laurel, I wasn't totally truthful with you."

He paused and her heart sank. "I did suspect that Johanna was doing drugs, and I tried to get her help. When she refused to go into a rehab facility, I went to Ben. He told me we had to be careful how we handled it to avoid bad publicity for the firm. I should have handled it."

Kase walked to her kitchenette, then came back.

"Maybe if I had pushed harder, I could have gotten Johanna into rehab."

Laurel had to stop this. "You put your trust in Ben to help his daughter. He failed her."

"But I was her husband. I should have made sure she was cared for."

"She refused your help, Kase. Johanna was an adult. You couldn't force her."

"I know. That's why I filed for the divorce, and I was going to get Addy, too. I would have never left her with her mother if Mary Beth hadn't been there."

"Kase, you were a good father. The only thing you did was work hard. That's not enough to make a judge side with the Chappells."

"You didn't hear all the awful things the lawyer said about me. What if I am a terrible father?"

"Why don't you ask your little girl that question? Who just happens to think you can do no wrong. Where is Addy anyway?"

"Gus is getting around better, and he sent me off to see you. Said he was tired of my bad mood."

Whatever the reason, she was so happy he was here. She leaned in and kissed him. "So how do I get rid of your bad mood?"

"Darlin', just being here with you brightens my mood. I missed you. After three days together, I hate us being apart."

"I missed you, too."

He pulled her close, resting his forehead against hers. "What are we going to do about that?"

"I don't know. You have any ideas?"

"Maybe a few." His mouth closed over hers. His taste was potent and familiar on her lips, only making her crave more. Her body ached with need for him. She ran her fingers through his hair, wanting to deepen the kiss.

"I want you so much." He broke off and swung her up into his arms, carrying her to the bed.

"I was only planning to steal a couple of kisses, but I ache for you, Laurel. So if you don't want me to stay, tell me now."

She touched his face. "I don't want you to leave, Kase."

At that moment, there wasn't anything more perfect than being with this man. She just didn't know how to keep the rest of the world out.

Chapter Thirteen

Before dawn the next morning, Laurel rolled over in her bed and read the clock. It was 4:37 a.m. She also noticed the other side of the bed was empty. Kase was gone? Sadness washed over her as she sat up and looked around the dark apartment.

"Looking for me?" She heard the familiar voice and smiled as Kase stepped out of the kitchenette. With two coffee mugs in his hand, he walked to the bed. "Good morning, sunshine."

She pulled the blanket closer around her body. "Good morning to you, too." She took the mug. "I thought you left."

He leaned down and kissed her gently on the lips. "Not before I said goodbye." He kissed her again, deeper, making her hungry for him.

He pulled back with a groan. "As much as I'd like to stay, I have chores to do, and Addy will be up soon."

"Of course, you need to get home to her," she told him. "Go."

He paused a moment, then said, "Come back to the house with me. Spend the day with us."

Sure, it wasn't as if she didn't have a business to run. "I've spent days with you, Kase. The last three days in fact. This morning, I have a full day of training scheduled."

He nodded. "What about the rest of the week?"

"I go to work at the accounting office tomorrow, but by next week, I'll be done because tax season is over." She'd already lost some hours during her trip to Denver. She hated not getting the extra money, then she remembered the envelope in her dresser.

"Laurel?"

She blinked and looked at Kase. "What?"

"Is something bothering you? I know I've been pressing for your time."

She liked being pushed.

When he started to move away from the bed, she reached for him. "No, it's not that. I loved our trip to Denver. It's just I need to think about my commitments. To be honest, I need the money that I make from the accounting firm."

He frowned. "To pay back your parents?"

With her nod, he said, "If it's that important, I have some money."

She stiffened. "Don't go there, Kase." She reached for her nightshirt beside the bed and slipped it on, then stood. "This is something I need to do myself." She went to her dresser, turned on the lamp, then opened the top drawer. "Seems someone else wants to help me, too. This came right before we left for Denver." She handed him the envelope.

Kase opened the package and pulled out the paper along with the stack of bills. "What the hell?"

"There's five thousand dollars."

He glared at her. "Is this from Aldrich?"

She shrugged. "It doesn't say, but I'm pretty sure it is."

"When did you say you got this?"

Okay, he was going to be angry. "The day we left on the trip."

She watched his eyes narrow. "I didn't tell you because you had enough on your mind with the court hearing. I thought I'd wait until we got home."

He ran his fingers through his hair. "I wish you'd told me sooner. I could have had the PI look into this. At the very least, let the police know about it."

"Jack's name isn't on this note, or the envelope. If it was, I would have contacted the police myself."

"Of course this is from Jack. Do you know anyone else who would send you five thousand dollars?"

Okay, now she was angry. "Look, I'm not on trial here, Kase, so stop acting like a lawyer." She waved her hand at him. "Take it, do what you want. I don't care." She turned away so he couldn't see how upset she was.

"Look, Laurel…"

She raised her hand to stop him. "We said enough. I need to get ready for work."

He wouldn't give up. "I don't want you to go through this alone." He touched her shoulder, and she shrugged it off.

She wheeled around. "I got into this mess. I'm the one who trusted Jack, and look what happened."

"When we fall in love, we don't always think clearly. You only trusted the wrong man."

When he came toward her, she backed away.

The last thing she wanted was to discuss her bad judgment. "Please, Kase. Let's just drop this."

He frowned but finally nodded. "I'm not stopping the investigation, so I'll take the envelope with me."

"Whatever you want to do with it. I don't want that money. Goodbye, Kase."

"Goodbye." He hesitated, then turned and walked out the door.

Laurel was shaking by the time she heard the door close, and then the footsteps on the stairs.

She wanted to call him back, but she couldn't add to his own burden. Now it looked like that was exactly what she had done.

For two long days, Kase wanted to see Laurel. He missed her smile, her touch, just being together. Addy missed her, too, and couldn't understand why her friend hadn't come to see her. What made it worse was Kase still hadn't heard anything from the judge about Addy's case.

Since he couldn't do anything about the custody decision, he concentrated on helping Laurel. He'd been in contact with the Denver police and faxed them a copy of the envelope with the PO box number and told them about the money.

He'd learned the mailbox didn't belong to Aldrich, but to a woman named Peggy Watson, Aldrich's ex-wife. The police also went through security tapes at that post office branch, but they showed only a man who could be Aldrich. So Kase had his PI stake out the branch, hoping old Jack would show up again. There wasn't much else he could do.

He wanted to tell Laurel of his plans, but when he'd called her, it went straight to voice mail. Okay, she was angry with him. He didn't blame her. He should have handled things better.

"Why don't you get in the car and go see her?"

Kase looked up to see his father come in the back door. "Who?"

"The woman you've been brooding about since you came home." He shook his head and limped to the kitchen sink. "I can't understand why anyone wastes their time arguing with a beautiful woman. Just tell her you're sorry. Better yet, send her flowers."

"Laurel didn't tell me about money that Jack sent her. She said she didn't want to burden me with her troubles."

Gus wiped his hands on a towel. "I just think she cares enough about you to keep her troubles to herself."

"Okay, so I worry about her. This Aldrich isn't a good guy. If he came back…"

"Give Laurel credit. She can handle herself. And if you care about her as much as you act like you do, then be there for her. Just don't try to run her life."

"I think I'm beginning to understand that. I just need to get her to talk to me so I can apologize."

"I tell you, flowers are the way to go."

LATER THAT DAY, Laurel paced the hospital waiting room along with her dad and mom. They'd been here the past four hours, ever since Trent had called to say that Brooke had gone into labor. She was three weeks early. The doctor wasn't too concerned, but Laurel couldn't help but worry for her sister and her little nephew. But at the thought of being an aunt, joy rushed through her.

She sent up a prayer asking God to take care of both of them. Christopher was being named after Trent's younger brother, who'd died in a riding accident when he was only nine. Trent had always felt responsible for not keeping Chris with him. It had been Brooke's love that helped her husband get rid of the guilt and ease the loss.

Trent came into the room dressed in green scrubs. He should have looked ridiculous, but the big ex-military man pulled it off. "The show's about to start. Brooke's progressing pretty quickly."

That brought smiles, and more tension. "Give her our

love, son," Rory said. "Tell her...we're here praying for her and the baby."

With a nod, Trent turned to Laurel and she whispered, "Tell Brooke I love her and can't wait to meet my nephew."

"I will." Trent hurried back into the birthing room.

Laurel had been in the room with Brooke earlier that day, but the birth of her baby should be shared only between Brooke and her husband.

Laurel felt a tightening around her heart. Would she ever be blessed with her own child? Her thoughts turned to Addy and tears formed in her eyes. She knew that she could love that little girl like she was her own, and felt the same about Kase. Darn. Why couldn't life be simple?

Two days seemed to be forever. And she missed him. She'd tried to concentrate on training Ruby Ridge, but she found her mind would wander to Kase. She checked her phone, afraid to take his calls. Now she was more frightened because his calls had stopped today.

Maybe she should call him and tell him about Brooke. She started to punch in the number when she heard her name.

"Laurel?"

She turned to see the man who'd been the center of her dreams for far too many nights. Dressed in a collared white shirt, creased jeans and polished boots, he walked toward her. Her heart began racing to the familiar rhythm whenever Kase was around.

"Kase. What are you doing here?"

He looked disappointed by her question. He paused. "I heard about Brooke, and I wanted to see if you or your family needed anything. I don't want to intrude."

He came all this way for her? "You aren't intruding

at all." She gripped his arm. "I'm glad you're here. It's been rough just waiting."

He arched an eyebrow. "So there's no word?"

"Trent came out a few minutes ago and said she was progressing."

"Would you like me to wait with you?"

Tears filled her eyes and she nodded. "I would like that."

He didn't hesitate and pulled her into a tight embrace. "Oh, Laurel, I'm so sorry I got angry with you. I know I hurt your feelings." He rubbed his hands up and down her back. "Your work is important. Your reputation as a horse trainer is incredible." His gaze locked on hers. "I guess I'm just a man who happens to want to be with you, a lot."

Laurel relished in his touch, his comfort. She needed this man so much it frightened her. "And maybe I over-reacted a little, too."

He touched her chin so she would look at him. "Why don't we talk about this later?" He kissed her gently, then nodded to the audience behind her. "When we're alone."

Laurel turned and faced her family. With Kase's nudge, they went to join them. He reached out and shook hands with her dad. Mom beamed. "It's good to see you, Kase."

"Nice to see you, too, Diane. I bet you're excited at becoming a grandma."

"Oh, yes. I can't wait to get my hands on little Chris."

Kase smiled. "I don't want to intrude with the family, but if you need me for anything, I'm here."

Rory spoke up. "You can hurry up that grandson of mine. He's taking far too long."

Kase chuckled. "I wish I could, but babies come when they're ready."

Rory nodded, then looked from Kase to his daughter. Although Laurel was an adult, she wanted her parents' approval.

"I'm glad you're here for Laurel," her dad told him.

Kase nodded. "I wouldn't be anywhere else."

Suddenly the door opened and Trent came in with a big grin. "Poppy and Mimi, and Aunt Laurel, Christopher Wade Landry has arrived." He blinked at tears as his voice grew hoarse with emotion. "My son is seven pounds and six ounces of all boy."

Laurel and her mother gasped and hurried to congratulate the new daddy.

"How is Brooke?" Diane asked.

"She's wonderful. And a champ in my book."

"Can we see her?" Laurel asked, still hanging on to Kase's hand.

"Give the doctor a few minutes. I'm going back in with my son while they clean him up. I don't want to miss anything." He walked back into the room.

Twenty minutes later, they went in to see Brooke. Rory was the first to hold his grandson, then Diane took a turn and cooed over the infant, who looked just like his daddy.

"I haven't even finished the baby quilt," Diane said. "Oh, and the baby shower is next week," she told Brooke.

"I think we can deal with the change in schedule." Brooke squeezed Diane's hand. "The most important thing, Chris is healthy. I want him to know his family, especially his grandparents."

Diane blinked back the tears forming in her eyes. When Brooke first arrived at the Bucking Q, Diane hadn't wanted Rory's *other* daughter around. She'd felt Brooke was a threat to her family. Over the months, they'd come to care about each other.

"And his Aunt Laurel." Diane handed the swaddled

baby to Laurel. The tiny baby felt wonderful in her arms. She fought tears as she examined the precious child. His dark eyes and crop of black hair looked like Trent's. She gripped his hand. "He's beautiful."

Kase stood close and looked over her shoulder. Laurel couldn't help but picture them as a family with maybe another child in their future.

AFTER LEAVING THE HOSPITAL, Laurel followed Kase back to his house. She was tired, but she promised to stop by and see Addy. It had been nearly three days since she'd seen the child. So when she got out of her car she felt excitement when Addy came rushing out the door dressed in her pink princess pajamas.

The child hurried down the steps, calling her name. "Laurel! Laurel! You came to see me."

Laurel caught the child in a big hug. She felt the warm weight and powdery scent that was only Addy's. "Hi, Addy. Of course I came to see you." She set her down on the porch steps. "I'm sorry, but I had to get some work done. I took time off to go with you to Denver and my horses missed me."

"Were they sad when you were gone?"

"Yes, but Wind wasn't being nice, either, so I had to spend extra time with him so he'd behave again."

Wide-eyed, she asked, "What'd he do?"

"Well, he kicked out one of the boards in his stall, then bucked off one of my trainers."

"Oh, no. Did he get a time-out?"

"Yes, he did. He's doing so much better now, so he gets apples and hugs for rewards when he's a good boy."

Laurel glanced at Kase. This was a delicate subject because of Addy's mother's harsh discipline. "Addy, I would never hit a horse, or anyone. I train my horses by telling and showing them how much I love them."

"I know. Chet said you have the magic touch with horses. You have them eating out of your hand." She giggled. "That's silly because that's how you feed them."

She was touched that Chet would say that. "Well, I love what I do."

She looked up at Kase and smiled. "Hey, Addy, did your daddy tell you that Brooke had her baby?"

She pouted. "I want to go see him, but Daddy said Chris is too little."

Laurel remembered her mother's invitation. "Yes, we have to be careful when babies are really small so they don't get sick. But there's going to be a party for the baby this weekend. If it's okay with your daddy, I'll take you."

Addy turned toward her father. "Please, Daddy, can I go?"

"If you go to bed without arguing, then yes, you can go for a little while."

"Okay." She stood and cheered, then hugged Laurel and her dad and went to the door. She paused, then asked, "Laurel, will you come up and read me a story?"

There was that tug on her heart. "Of course. Go brush your teeth and get into bed."

The child started to leave again when her grandfather came out. She kissed him, too, then disappeared.

"My, that girl hasn't moved that fast in days." Gus smiled. "Nice to see you, Laurel."

"How have you been?"

"Getting around," Gus said as he held open the door and Kase and Laurel walked into the kitchen. "While you all have been gallivanting around Denver, I've been here working."

Kase smiled. "You're just upset because you aren't the center of attention since you got back on your feet."

Laurel noticed that he was standing on his own. "Oh, look at you, Gus. You aren't using a cane, or anything."

The older man beamed, even stood a little taller. "I'm not doing too bad, for an old guy. I'm still in physical therapy, but soon I'll be back on a horse."

Kase finally spoke up. "Let's table that until we talk to the doctor. You don't want to rush it."

"I didn't say I was going riding tomorrow." Gus huffed, then smiled again at Laurel. "I better head to bed myself. Good night, Laurel. Don't be a stranger."

Laurel went over and hugged the man. "I won't."

Once Gus left the kitchen, Kase reached for Laurel and drew her close as he leaned against the counter. "I've missed you so much." He bent down and kissed her. "Again, I'm sorry about the other day."

"That's over." She kissed his chin, loving the feeling of being in his arms. And as much as she ached to get lost in his loving, they had too many other distractions. "Come on. We have a little girl waiting for us."

She took his hand and together they went upstairs to Addy's room. It took only about ten minutes of reading, and a short discussion of what to buy baby Christopher, before the four-year-old yawned, then rolled on her side and closed her eyes. Seemed all was right in her world. If only life were that simple.

Laurel kissed Addy's cheek, wishing she could always be included in this child's nightly ritual. With one last look at the sleeping child, she and Kase walked out of the room.

Kase waited in the hall as Laurel closed Addy's door. As much as he wanted to take her into his bedroom and let her know how much he'd missed her these past days, the safest place for them to have their talk was downstairs.

He directed her back into the kitchen so they wouldn't disturb Gus in the den. He pulled out a ladder-back chair and she sat down, then he joined her. He hated to wreck the mood, but he needed to tell her about Aldrich.

"I heard from my PI."

Laurel sat up straighter. "You found Jack?"

Kase shook his head. "Not yet, but the PO box address belongs to his ex-wife."

"His ex-wife?"

"You didn't know he'd been married?"

"Of course I did," she said, then added, "since Trent looked into Jack's background last fall. But I doubt if anyone went looking for her. What's her name?"

"Peggy Watson. She still lives in Denver and has the same PO box, which I believe Jack has a key to—or maybe he never gave it back to her."

Laurel rubbed her temples. "This just keeps getting better." Her gaze avoided his. "Don't say it. I should have learned more about the man I'd planned to marry. Please tell me they aren't still married."

He wasn't going to mention she was far too trusting. "They were divorced three years ago. I'm still trying to understand why Jack put a return address on the envelope. He should have known that law enforcement would trace it." Kase suddenly knew the answer. "Unless…he wants you to get in contact with him."

"That's crazy. If he wanted me around, why'd he leave?"

"From what we've discovered, he had no choice but to take Rory's money to pay off a gambling debt."

"He's not going to like it if I ever get my hands on him."

"No, Laurel. I don't want you anywhere near him. Promise me that if he contacts you again, you'll let us know."

"But if I can get him to give me more money…"

He shook his head. "We don't know what else Jack is involved in. Illegal gambling…money laundering… And those guys can play for keeps." He went to her and pulled her to her feet. He didn't want anything to happen to her. "Please, promise me you aren't going to do anything foolish."

"I'm not stupid, Kase."

He raised a soothing hand. "I'm sorry. I just don't want you to worry so much about getting the money from Jack that he manages to talk you into seeing him."

She shook her head as tears filled her eyes. "I never should have trusted him, but he told me he loved me." Her voice softened. "But he knew I didn't love him, not that way. We were both lonely. One night after a few drinks we got this crazy notion…"

"To get married?"

She eyed him closely. "I guess you weren't the only one who chose the wrong person."

He didn't want to remember the turmoil that Johanna had put him through. "Why didn't you just wait to fall in love with someone?"

Laurel met his gaze. "Because I was already in love with someone, but he didn't want me."

Chapter Fourteen

The following Sunday afternoon, Kase drove to the Bucking Q Ranch to deliver an excited little girl for Brooke's baby shower. He climbed out of his SUV, opened the back door, released Addy's safety seat and helped her down.

They were a little early for the party, but Kase didn't want to be there when the other guests showed up. That included a lot of women, since men weren't invited to the party. He'd been instructed by Trent to drop off Addy, then meet the other guys at Q and L cabin number one. The other husbands and boyfriends would be there to celebrate the birth of Chris.

"Daddy, how do I look?"

He glanced down at his adorable daughter dressed in a ruffled white skirt and a pink shirt that read Pretty in Pink and white sneakers with glittery laces.

"You look beautiful, sweetie."

She smiled and his heart tripped. She was the joy of his life, and losing her would kill him. He couldn't imagine not having his daughter with him.

"Daddy, did you hear me?"

He shook away the dark thought. "What, sweetie?"

"I said, do you think Christopher will like the horsey?"

"Of course. Every little boy wants a horse. Come on, you've got a party to go to." Together they walked around to the back of the car and lifted the hatch. The gift might be a little extravagant, but when Addy saw the wooden horse in the store window, she wouldn't settle for anything else.

Kase lifted the horse from the back and along with his daughter walked up the steps and knocked on the back door. After hearing "Come in," he allowed Addy in first, then followed her into the kitchen.

Laurel was busy at the sink, her back to them. There were trays of small fancy sandwiches and a big bowl of green salad on the table. Laurel turned and smiled. "Addy and Kase, you're here."

He wanted nothing more than to walk across the room, take her in his arms and plant a big kiss on her inviting mouth. He tabled that thought until later. "I thought I'd drop Addy off a little early, along with this guy."

"And sneak out," Laurel teased as she walked over and hugged Addy. "Don't you look adorable."

The four-year-old smiled. "You look pretty, too."

Kase thought so, too. Navy trouser pants and a print blue-and-burgundy tunic-style top with a wide belt showed off her small waist.

"I agree," he told her.

Laurel gave quick kisses to both of them. "Oh, my, that's a big horse. Let's take it in with the other presents and the other early guests."

He groaned and followed as she led them through the Quinns' formal dining room. A lace tablecloth covered the table with a big bouquet of flowers as a centerpiece, blue napkins and plates and matching balloons, one that announced "It's a Boy." In the living room there were already several women on the other side of the room, busy looking at the baby in the bassinette.

He hadn't seen Chris since the hospital, but he planned

to keep it that way for now. He wanted a quick departure from the party. He found the stack of presents on the fireplace hearth and placed the horse down. He kissed Addy and instructed her that he'd be back to pick her up in a few hours.

He took Laurel aside in the doorway to the dining room. "Thank you for inviting Addy today. She's been so excited all week."

"I'm glad. There are a few other little girls coming, too. So she'll have someone to play with."

Kase wasn't hearing anything Laurel said. He was thinking about how much he wanted to steal her away. "I should go. I'll be with Trent and your dad at the cabin if you need me."

"You don't want to see Chris?"

He would love to hold the little guy. "He's a little busy right now. I'll wait until later when I pick up Addy."

"See you then." Laurel kissed him sweetly, then she started to push him toward the door.

When he heard the collective gasp over her action, he said, "I'm out of here." He turned and walked through the kitchen and out the door.

Laurel smiled, her heart still pounding wildly, watching Kase leave. She fought the urge to go after him. Instead, she turned her focus to the group of women who came today to celebrate the birth of her nephew, Christopher.

Her mother, Diane, had helped with the party. Trent's mother, Leslie Landry Brannigan, came from Denver to see her first grandson, and the namesake of her son Christopher. She hadn't returned to Hidden Springs since she'd divorced her first husband, Wade. Their marriage hadn't survived after they'd lost their youngest son.

The new mother, Brooke, was dressed in a sheath-style blue print dress and looked wonderful for having a baby a week ago. Next to her was their biological mother, Coralee Harper, who had early onset Alzheimer's and lived in a facility in town.

Another friend of Brooke's, Erin Carlton, had been Coralee's caretaker in Las Vegas and recently relocated here to work as a nurse. Erin was the reason Coralee could be here today. The older woman was a little confused over the party and her new grandson, but Brooke wanted her here, and to take pictures to mark the occasion.

Little Addy went over to the rocking horse and announced, "This is my present for baby Christopher for being born."

The group chuckled.

"And it's lovely," Diane said. "Don't you think so, Leslie?"

The two women had been friends over forty years from way back when their husbands, Wade and Rory, traveled the rodeo circuit. Later they had also been neighbors.

Laurel hadn't seen the former Mrs. Landry since she was a little girl. Leslie's blond hair was now streaked with gray and were a few more lines around her pretty blue eyes, but Laurel remembered her sweet smile. Leslie made her way to the rocking horse.

"He's beautiful," she told Addy.

"I know, and I thought baby Christopher would really like him. This can be his first horse till he's old enough and gets a real one. I named him Buckeye."

The room grew silent, knowing that had been the name of Leslie's son's horse.

"Laurel said Christopher's uncle's favorite thing in the whole world was his horse." The little girl cocked her head sideways and looked at Leslie. "Maybe Uncle Chris will see him from heaven and smile."

Addy looked at Laurel. She was barely holding it together, but she managed to nod.

Leslie finally spoke up. "Thank you, Addy, for the lovely gift. Now we have a reminder of Chris's horse." She hugged the child. "You brought the best present ever."

Diane took Addy's hand and together they walked over to the baby.

Addy looked into the white bassinette with the blue lining, staring at the baby. "He looks like my baby dolly."

Smiling, Laurel looked down at the infant. Christopher was the image of Trent. He had dark hair and his big brown eyes were wide as several women cooed over him.

Laurel had fallen hopelessly in love with her nephew, making her want a child of her own even more. Her thoughts turned to Kase. Back in high school they'd daydreamed about getting married and having a houseful of kids. Was that all it was, a dream?

Hearing Addy's voice, Laurel quickly returned to the present. "He keeps waving his arms. It's like he's waving to us."

"I think he hears your voice and is excited you're here."

Addy turned her face to Laurel and smiled. "I'm excited I got to come to the party."

Beaming with pride, Brooke walked over to them. "We're glad you came, too. You look so pretty in your pink shirt. That's my favorite color on you."

Addy looked down at her outfit. "I picked out my prettiest clothes because it's a special party." The child looked at Laurel. "Daddy said you were the prettiest girl in high school."

Laurel tried not to blush but lost the effort. "Thank you, sweetie."

She was happy when the doorbell rang and more guests arrived, including two little girls who came with their mother.

With Addy distracted, Laurel returned to the kitchen to finish the food prep. Yet she couldn't help but think about Kase. She'd missed him this past week, but they both had things to do, and Laurel wanted to catch up with her training schedule and needed to get the baby shower together.

Yet the man wasn't far from her mind. The picture of the two of them together had Laurel dreaming not only of a life with Kase, but also Addy. She loved them both, but how did Kase feel about a future for all of them?

AT THE CABIN, Kase sat back in an overstuffed chair with a longneck bottle in his hand. He'd been nursing the same beer for the past hour. The other men were a lot further along than he was, but he wasn't about to try to catch up.

He was distracted, his thoughts on Laurel. He wanted to be with her, now and in the future. He'd been a fool to let her walk away, and he was going to do everything to keep it from happening a second time. He needed her in his life.

He glanced around the one-bedroom cabin on the Quinn property that usually rented out for fishing and hunting. The four other rental cabins were a nice way to bring in extra income for both Rory and Trent. Trent was also hired on as an outfitter frequently. There were plans to build more and expand the business to include more structures for country weddings and business retreats.

His own head was spinning with ideas for the Rawlins Horse Ranch. Dad was doing well with his new hip and eager to start training again.

He wanted to move on with his life, too. Make more improvements at the ranch—the barn and corral needed help—and hire some help for the chores. Even the house was desperate for repairs. Maybe he could add on an addition to the main floor, and a new kitchen. A place a woman would feel comfortable living in.

Suddenly laughter broke out and he heard his name. "Isn't that true, Rawlins?" Trent asked. "Aren't girls harder to raise than boys?"

Kase smiled. "They might be, but I wouldn't trade my little girl for anything."

"She's a little heartbreaker, that one," Rory added with a grin. Rory would make a much better grandfather than Ben Chappell any day.

Trent glanced at the time. "I wonder if the ladies are finished with the party."

"Why, are you that eager to go back and change diapers?" one of the men teased.

Trent nodded. "I spent a lot of years wiping the bottoms of recruits, so taking care of my son is nothing but a joy. Brooke and Chris are the best things that have ever happened to me."

Kase stood and raised his bottle. "To fatherhood." Then it suddenly hit him that his family was all he needed to be happy. That included Laurel.

AFTER THE BABY SHOWER, Laurel walked upstairs at her parents' house and peeked into her old bedroom. She smiled, finding Addy fast asleep in the bed. The girl had had a busy day.

Laurel turned to see Kase walking toward her. Before she could speak, he reached her, and then without even a hello, he was kissing her.

Oh, mercy. The man had skills. He knew how to hit

the right buttons. With the firm pressure of his mouth on hers, she tasted him. Inhaled his scent and her desire grew.

He hooked his arms around her back and drew her closer. She was plastered right up against him until she couldn't think of anything else. Soon he maneuvered her against the wall. Oh, boy, she was melting on the spot.

She managed to come to her senses and broke off the kiss. Trying to gather her breath, she glanced down the hall, hoping her parents weren't around.

"Sorry, I can't stop myself around you." He cupped her face and whispered, "I want you so much, Laurel."

She knew how he felt. "I want you, too," she admitted.

He rested his forehead against hers. "I'm trying to be good. What I really want to do is carry you off to one of those vacant hunting cabins."

Laurel wanted to tell him she'd like that, too, when he surprised her and asked, "How would you like to go out on a date tonight?"

"With you and Addy?"

He shook his head. "Just you and me as a couple. No kids allowed." He pressed a soft kiss on her lips. She wanted him to linger longer.

"I love that idea, but I probably should help Mom and Leslie with cleanup." Leslie was staying here at the house while in town.

Kase shook his head. "Both women were in the kitchen having coffee. The place was spotless. I guess your services aren't needed tonight." He paused and pulled her close. "So, Miss Quinn, how would you like to go out with me tonight?"

Before she got too excited, she nodded toward the bedroom. "What about Addy?"

"Got that covered, too. Your mother said she'd watch

her tonight." He nuzzled her neck, causing shivers to rush down her spine. "Come on, your choice on where to go. Dinner, a movie, dancing…"

Laurel pulled back and looked into his mesmerizing gray eyes. She wanted desperately to be alone with this man. "I know where the extra keys to the cabins are."

LATER THAT EVENING, in the queen-size bed at the cabin, Kase pulled Laurel closer against his side and covered them with a blanket.

"I don't want to move ever again," she breathed as she placed her arm across his chest. "I'm happy to stay here forever."

He rubbed his fingers over her arm. He wanted the same thing. But how did they keep the outside world from intruding?

As badly as he wanted to plan a future with this woman, how could he when he didn't know what tomorrow would bring?

Laurel raised her head, her blond hair highlighted in the dimly lit bedroom. "I can hear you thinking, or should I say worrying?"

He hugged her closer, feeling her warm, sexy body against him. "I'm sorry. I wanted to give you my undivided attention."

She smiled and something squeezed around his heart. "You were doing a pretty good job a few minutes ago." Her green eyes darkened with desire. "I've never made love—"

He stopped her words with a finger to her lips. "I don't want to hear about any other men in your life." He'd never been the jealous type, until Laurel. "You can keep them in your past."

She gripped his finger, then kissed it. "You don't have to worry, Kase. You're the best lover I've ever had."

"Damn right, I am."

He couldn't help but grin, then flipped her over onto her back. She giggled and he kissed her, then kissed her again until they were both groaning.

"And here I was worrying that any minute your father would come banging on the door, wanting to know my intentions."

"I'm an adult, Kase. I can do what I want without my parents' permission."

He sobered. "I still don't like sneaking around."

She grinned. "Really? You don't think it was a little exciting stumbling around in the dark, feeling our way from the front door and into the bed?"

"Well, maybe I enjoyed it a little. Kind of reminded me of that time in high school when your dad caught us making out in my truck."

"Oh, yeah." She blew out a breath. "I got the *big* sex talk that night. Dad gave me the male point of view. What guys are really after."

"And what are guys really after?" he asked as he placed kisses along her neck and down to her breasts.

"The same thing girls are after." She raised his head to make him look at her. "It must have worked because I never had another lover since you."

He froze. How could that be? "What about…?" He couldn't get himself to say Aldrich's name.

She shook her head. "There's only been you."

They hadn't been together for ten years. "But you were engaged."

Laurel wiggled her delicious body against him. "You really want to hear the details when you're in bed with a willing naked woman?"

He groaned. "God, no."

"Wise man." She wrapped her arms around his neck and pulled him down for a slow, deep kiss.

When he tore his mouth away, his gaze locked on hers. "I could get lost in you. In your eyes…your laughter… your mouth…your body…" His lips brushed over hers. "My feelings for you aren't just physical, Laurel. The way you make me feel…inside."

He stopped and swallowed back the raw emotions. Suddenly he realized he needed her as much as his next breath. "I don't want to lose you again."

Laurel reached out and touched his face. "Kase, I'm not going anywhere."

Chapter Fifteen

The next morning, Laurel hurried across the Allen and Jacobs Accounting parking lot. She'd gotten a surprise call from Mr. Allen asking her to come in to work today and tomorrow to finish up some accounts.

Although she had been sad to leave Kase last night, she'd talked with him this morning and offered to bring Addy home from school. So she'd get to see him then, too. They'd made a date to go out to dinner tomorrow evening, so this was a bonus.

Laurel walked through the glass office doors and greeted the receptionist. "Good morning, Melody."

"You sure are happy for a Monday morning," Melody said.

She was allowing herself to be happy about Kase, along with the extra money she was getting paid this week. "I had a great weekend. Brooke's baby shower was yesterday."

Melody smiled. "Oh, how is the little guy?"

Laurel couldn't help but act like a proud aunt. She took out her phone and brought up pictures of her nephew. "Chris is adorable, and he's growing so fast."

"Gosh, he's so cute," Melody cooed, "But, hey, look at his parents. They're both gorgeous."

Laurel beamed. "Since Brooke is my twin sister, I'll

take that as a compliment. Thank you. Now, I better get to work. Mr. Allen said he'd leave my work packet with you."

Melody went through her files, then she finally came up with a thick manila envelope. "Here it is." She handed the packet over. "Have a good morning."

"You, too."

Laurel walked down the hall to the familiar glass-enclosed work cubicle. After putting her purse away in the drawer, she sat down and turned on the computer. As the machine warmed up, she opened the envelope and took out the small stack of client files. She scanned the top four accounts and their instructions, then she came to the last file. On the front page it read Kase Augustus Rawlins. She froze. She wasn't sure if she should have this. Wasn't Mr. Allen personally handling Kase's account?

Okay, what she needed to do was put this file aside and not look at it. She hesitated. Then curiosity got the best of her and she opened the file folder. Without getting a chance to see the bottom line of Kase's net worth, she saw the Post-it addressed to Cleve Allen from one of the senior accountants in the office.

Cleve,
In trying to transfer Addison Marie Rawlins's trust account from Denver, I was unsuccessful. I did manage to obtain the balance of the account. It was substantially less than what was estimated by Mr. Rawlins.
Mike Henderson.

Laurel saw the date and noticed the report came in on Friday. Okay, what should she do? She had to look, of course. She opened the file of Addy's portfolio. With a quick glance over the lists of stocks and bonds, she went straight to the bottom line. She raised an eyebrow. This was a lot of money, or was it? Then she saw the number of withdrawals and gasped. Why would someone take money out of a child's account?

As if a lightbulb went off, she smiled at her conclusion. This could change everything.

THE MORNING DRAGGED on as Kase went about his morning chores. He'd dropped off Addy at preschool, but he really missed her chatter and company. Now he was looking forward to her coming home, along with Laurel bringing her from town.

His two girls. He liked the sound of that. If only he could convince Laurel to stay the day. These late spring days had him thinking about new beginnings. He wanted a fresh start with his daughter, and hopefully with Laurel. He still couldn't get over his surprise at her confession. He'd been humbled to know he'd been her only lover.

Not even her fiancé. He didn't want to think about Aldrich, but as long as he was out there, he was trouble for Laurel. He didn't like knowing Jack could show up at Laurel's door anytime. No, Jack Aldrich needed to be found, and soon.

Kase walked through the barn toward Honor's Promise's stall. He couldn't help but smile. Something was going right. "Hey, girl, how are you doing today?"

With an excited whinny, the pretty chestnut came up to the gate to meet him, putting her muzzle against his chest, wanting some attention. It had been nearly two months since Capture the Wind had broken down the fence and mounted his mare. That same day Laurel came barreling back into his life. Now he was going to try everything he could to keep her there.

"How's she doing?"

Kase turned to see his dad. There was only a slight limp in his gait as Gus made his way toward them.

Kase scratched the mare's neck. "The vet checked her earlier. She's happy and healthy. Matt also told me about a bay stallion that's for sale over at the Phillipses' ranch. Seems Jake and Kitty are selling off their stock, leasing their grazing land and retiring to Arizona to be with their kids and grandkids."

Gus shook his head. "I'd heard rumors. Maybe we should go and check it out. All Jake's horses are registered stock."

Kase hesitated. "I'd like to."

His father studied him with a cautious eye. "What's on your mind, son?"

"Just hate all this waiting. I want to move forward, but I'm not sure I can. Not until I find out about the custody case. I might have to move back to Denver."

"Dammit. They can't take Addy away from us. Any judge has to see that little girl loves you, and you've done nothing that would jeopardize losing her."

Kase wasn't so sure. "I wasn't the best father in Addy's early years. I worked all the time, trying to build my career. I left her with a drug-addicted mother."

"From what you said, Addy had Mary Beth looking out for her."

"Maybe the judge thinks that having a woman in her life is better instead of a single dad."

"Bah." Gus waved his hand. "Then ask Laurel to marry you. She loves both you and Addy. And from what I can tell whenever she's around, you feel the same way. What are you waiting for, son?"

"If I lose Addy to the Chappells, I'll have to move back

to Denver just to be there for her. How can I ask Laurel to give up her family and life here?"

Gus took off his hat and scratched his head. "Don't think for her. Give her the choice."

He wanted nothing more than to include Laurel in his life. But everything was such a mess.

His father went on to say, "I made that mistake, and I couldn't undo it."

"Are you talking about my mother?"

Gus nodded. "She wanted me to move to the city. I refused, and she left me. I feel I cheated you out of your mother."

"No, Dad, you can't make excuses for Liz Rawlins. She left me, her child, all on her own. If I've learned any-thing in the past four years, you have to think about your child first. You were always there for me, and I know I haven't said it in a long time, but I love you." He blew out a breath. "Now I just pray that the judge doesn't side with Ben because of their social ties. I want the chance to be the father that Addy needs."

His dad's eyes welled with tears. "I pray that, too. That little girl has stolen my heart."

Before Kase could say any more, his cell phone rang. He saw the familiar number of his lawyer. He answered it reluctantly. "Sam, what's up?"

"Good morning to you, too."

"Sorry, good morning, Sam. Now please give me some good news."

"It's not good, it's not bad. I received news that the judge will render his decision."

"When?"

"Tomorrow afternoon. Four o'clock. Can you make that?"

Kase sighed, trying to slow his racing heart. "I guess I have no choice. Yes, I'll be there."

Sam paused, then said, "My instructions were to have you bring Addy, too."

Kase's heart sank into his stomach. Oh, God, no. They wouldn't take her away. "Okay, we'll be there."

His father saw his pain. "Not good news."

Kase shrugged. "Not sure what the judge decided, but they want me to bring Addy along to court tomorrow." He shook his head. "I can't give her up, Dad. What am I going to do?" He raked his hand through his hair. "If the judge sides with the Chappells, Addy will think I deserted her."

Gus caught his son in a tight hug. "Oh, son, Addy knows you love her," he whispered, his voice laced with emotion. "But hey, don't give up, the judge could decide in your favor."

Kase nodded. His dad was right. He needed to stay positive.

"Hey, we better pull ourselves together," Gus said. "Addy will be home anytime now."

"Yeah, I don't want to upset her." Kase rubbed the mare's nose one last time and he and his father walked out of the barn.

They were headed toward the house when Laurel's truck came up the road. "Looks like your ladies are home."

Kase put on a smile and pretended everything was fine. Laurel shut off the engine and climbed out.

"Hi there," he greeted her.

"Hi, yourself," she answered.

"Thanks for bringing Addy home."

"Not a problem." She smiled. "I need to talk to you anyway."

Kase nodded and opened the truck's back door and smiled at the sight of his daughter.

"Hi, Daddy. I had the best day at school. I made a new friend. His name is Michael, but he likes to be called Micky. And I colored a picture of you and Papa Gus and Laurel. And baby Chris on his new horse. It's in my backpack."

Kase swallowed. "Looks like you've been busy." He lifted her out of her seat and held on to her a little longer and a little tighter. He inhaled that sweet scent that was so uniquely Addy.

"Daddy, don't squeeze so hard."

He loosened his grip. "Sorry, sweetie, I just missed you so much today. Dr. Matt came out to see Honor and said the foal is growing in her tummy."

Addy grinned. "I can't wait to see the baby when it's born." Her blue eyes widened. "Can I name the new horsey?"

He nodded. "You bet." He handed her the backpack. "Now, you better go inside and see Papa. He's fixing you a snack."

The child took off, and once she was through the door, Kase reached for Laurel and pulled her into an embrace. He needed her to anchor him, to feel her support and strength. "I've missed you since last night."

She pulled back. "I missed you, too." She turned serious. "We need to talk, Kase."

He didn't like this. "Sure."

"Could we go into Gus's office?"

He nodded.

She took his hand. "Don't worry. For a change, this could be good news."

Laurel took his hand and walked into the house, where they found Gus and Addy seated at the kitchen table eating peanut butter crackers. "We'll be back in a minute or two. Laurel wants to discuss something with me."

His father gave him a wink. "Take your time, we're fine here."

Kase led her down the hall and into the den/office. After shutting the door, he took her in his arms. "First, I need this." His mouth lowered to hers, in hopes of escaping their troubles for a little while.

Laurel pulled away. "As much as I love your kisses, you're distracting me."

"Sounds like a great idea."

He hated to burden her with his problems, but he had to share. "I received a call from my lawyer right before you got here," he said. "The judge has made his decision. I have to go back to Denver tomorrow."

Laurel walked to the desk, set her purse down and took out a piece of paper. "I need to tell you something, Kase." She paused a long time and he got worried.

"Just tell me, Laurel."

"When I went into the office today, your financial file was given to me by mistake."

He shrugged and sat on the edge of the chair. "I don't mind if you saw it."

"Well, I didn't look anyway," she admitted. "But if you don't mind, could you tell me how much money Addy has in her trust?"

He wasn't expecting this question. "I'm not exactly sure."

"Just a round number would help."

He thought back to the last time he saw her trust account. "Okay, the last time I saw any documentation was right after Johanna died about a year ago. It was over two million, but of course with her mother's trust money added in from the heritance, I'm going to say a rough estimate would be five to six million according to how good the stock market is."

Laurel's eyes widened. "Oh, my. That much?"

He nodded. "None of it's my money. It's all safely tucked away for Addy when she turns twenty-five. Can I ask where this is going?"

She raised a hand. "Okay, I'll admit when your file was in front of me I was tempted to look at your worth. I guess I wanted to know how successful you were in Denver." She blushed. "Then I was distracted by a Post-it note from one of the senior accountants. The note was addressed to Mr. Allen saying there wasn't as much money in Addy's trust as you had told him." She unfolded the paper. "I'm not sure if this is unethical or not, but since Cleve Allen is out of town all week, I wanted you to have the news as soon as possible. You don't have time to wait, especially when you're going back to court tomorrow." She handed him the paper. "I brought you a copy of the spreadsheet that Mr. Allen would give to you anyway when he returns. Here is the amount of money in Addy's account now."

Kase took the paper and went straight to the bottom line, and saw the amount was just under $300,000. "Whoa. Something's wrong. There's a mistake. I have paperwork upstairs that shows a year ago the account had several million."

"Who else has access to the trust?"

"Not me. Ben Chappell is the executor."

Laurel's gaze locked on his. "This might be out of line, but do you think it's possible that your father-in-law has been illegally taking money from the trust?"

A flash went off in Kase's head. "Damn, that bastard. That has to be why Ben wants Addy. He stole her money." He finally grinned. He couldn't care less about the money, but with this information, he could keep Addy. He walked over and pulled Laurel into his arms and kissed her. "Thank you. Thank you. You have no idea what this means."

Laurel grinned, too. "You get to be Addy's full-time daddy?"

For the first time in months he had hope that he could have a life with his daughter. He looked at Laurel. Was it possible to have it all?

LATER THAT EVENING, an exhausted Laurel had finished her training with Ruby Ridge and was headed upstairs to her apartment. She'd been invited back to Kase's house for supper, but she'd declined, knowing how busy her day had been and how badly she needed some sleep.

Before she left Kase, she had him call Allen and Jacobs to get the official documents on the account. Then she'd be off the hook.

There was no doubt that Ben Chappell was involved, along with the bank that held the money. No one else had access to the funds. Now Addy didn't have to leave her father, and Kase didn't have to leave Hidden Springs. Maybe they all could have a future together.

Her cell phone rang. Her heart sank when she recognized the number. "Hello."

"Hello, Laurel. Did you get the money?"

She stiffened. "Jack. Where are you?"

"I just wanted to say I'm sorry and I hope you'll forgive me." Then the connection ended.

Great. She didn't need this today.

She heard a knock on the door and her heart pounded in her chest. "Oh, God, no. Please don't be Jack."

She looked through the peephole and was relieved to find Kase on the porch. She unlocked the door, opened it and didn't give him a chance to say anything before she launched herself into his arms.

"Wow, I like the greeting."

She was trembling. "Sorry. It just…" She held out her phone. "I got a call from Jack."

He stepped inside the apartment. "What the hell? When?"

"Just now. When I heard the knock, I thought it was him. He only said 'Did you get the money?' and 'I'm sorry.' Then he hung up."

Kase checked the number, then walked to the kitchenette and made a call to his PI to give him the information. "My guy is going to try to trace the number."

Laurel hated that her past kept causing trouble. "I'm sorry, Kase. You have enough on your mind right now."

He shook his head. "What are you talking about? It's thanks to you, for pointing out the deficit in Addy's account, my problems could be over. I don't think Ben can explain his way out of this. Even if he can, just my investigating into the loss of Addy's trust money will have his clients questioning his ethics. That could mean the demise of the law firm." Kase frowned. "I got a hold of Jacobs and he sent the entire account information to my lawyer. So we'll be prepared for court tomorrow."

"Was Mr. Jacobs upset that I gave you the information?"

"He doesn't know, Laurel. Even if he did, you didn't do anything illegal by giving me the account records. You caught the oversight. I wouldn't have learned about it until next week. By then, Ben could have been awarded custody of Addy."

She finally smiled. "I'm glad I could help."

He gave her a quick kiss. "Me, too."

"Now, I still have to go to Denver tomorrow. Sam

and I plan to meet with the Chappells and their lawyer. I want you to go with me, Laurel, mainly because I don't want Addy to be afraid. If you can watch her, I'm planning to confront Ben. What he did was embezzle money, and at the very least he could be disbarred and lose his law practice."

Laurel was curious. "I thought the Chappells were wealthy. Why would he need to take Addy's money?"

Kase shrugged. "First of all, Judith comes from money. The Kirsch family struck it big in gold nearly a century ago and invested wisely in many more enterprises over the years. Ben built his law practice himself, and he's done well for himself. But it's a large firm. You lose clients and their hefty retainers, and that can be a game changer. When I wanted to make partner, I was told over and over to bring clients into the firm. There's a lot of overhead with a high-rise downtown office."

"So are you going to send Ben to jail?"

Kase pulled her close. "I don't want that, but if I have no choice, I will. No one messes with my family."

Chapter Sixteen

The next day, Laurel got up at 5:00 a.m., did a few chores, let Chet know she'd be gone for the day and asked him to take over her training schedule.

She could see her foreman wanted to question her, but he only nodded and went on with his business. She knew she was putting her business second, but all she could think about was that Kase and Addy needed her. Everything else would have to wait.

After a quick shower, she dressed in dark jeans and a blue oxford cloth blouse. She doubted she had to do much more than watch Addy, so this outfit seemed the most practical. After grabbing a lightweight sweater, Laurel was waiting on her apartment steps when Kase drove up at six thirty.

When she heard Addy's fussy cries, she climbed in the backseat and kissed the child hello.

"Now, let's get you and your dollies comfortable." Laurel arranged the child's favorite blanket around the safety seat to support her head. She stroked Addy's arm and hummed one of her favorite songs until the child went back to sleep. Then there was silence in the car.

Kase reached a hand back and touched Laurel's knee. "Thank you," he whispered. "You're a miracle worker."

No, she just cared about this child. She leaned forward and said, "Addy is just afraid. She can see your worry."

"I guess I didn't do a very good job of hiding it, or preparing her for this trip. Damn Ben," he hissed. "How could he put her through this?"

Laurel placed her hand on Kase's, loving the connection to this man. She hoped he knew how much she loved his child. "Hopefully, today will put an end to that worry and you can move ahead with your lives."

His gaze met hers in the rearview mirror. "I hope you know I want you involved in those decisions, too."

Laurel wanted that, too. She wanted to dream about a future with Kase and Addy. But there were still many things that needed to be resolved. "Why don't we table this discussion? You need to concentrate on today."

"Not for too long, Laurel. I'm tired of living in limbo." He turned his attention back to his driving.

Laurel tried to nap like Addy, but she couldn't seem to stop thinking about a possible future with Kase. Could it really happen?

There were things still standing in her way. She needed to repay her parents and Trent. Although Trent and Rory both told her she wasn't responsible, she knew she was the one who'd given Jack the password to the escrow account. Her father entrusted her with the finances of the project, and she screwed up big-time.

ONCE THEY ARRIVED in Denver, Kase took them to Emma's Café, just walking distance from the courthouse. Best part, Addy was happily distracted coloring the picture on the kids' menu. He looked across the table to watch Laurel avoid eye contact. Maybe he was conjuring up problems, but something was bothering her.

"Laurel, what's wrong?"

She shook her head, then glanced down at the child next to her. "Just want this over with. I think we'd all feel better."

Kase blew out a breath and glanced at his daughter. He wanted Addy's happiness above everything else. For the first time since this custody battle began, he felt they might be able to start building a life in Hidden Springs.

He took her hand in his. "I want that, too." His cell phone went off. "It's Sam." He read the text. "He wants to meet with me."

Kase texted him back. At Emma's Café.

Sam replied, B there in 5 minutes.

"He's coming here." He glanced at Laurel. "I don't want to take Addy to the courthouse just yet. Maybe I should have gotten a hotel room."

Laurel shook her head. "We've only a few hours to wait," she said, keeping her voice in a quiet tone. "If it takes longer, I can always take Addy shopping, or even go visit the aquarium again."

"Yeah, Daddy, I like the aquarium. I like to color, too. See my picture?" She held it up. "I was careful to stay inside the lines." She smiled. "At school, my teacher said I did a good job and she gave me a star."

"Great job, sweetie."

Kase knew he couldn't keep hiding things from his daughter. If they could just get through today without a lot of drama… "Addy, I have to go back into court today and see your grandfather."

Those big blue eyes locked on his, and his chest tightened. "I know, Daddy. Grandpa wants me to live with him and Grandma." She shook her head. "I don't want to. I want to live with you. You tell him that, okay? Then we can go home to live forever and ever with Papa Gus and Laurel and Pops and Mimi."

He didn't know what he did to deserve this child, but he couldn't let her down. "You're going home with me today, guaranteed," he emphasized.

His child grinned.

He glanced at Laurel to see tears in her eyes. He took hold of her hand. "It's going to be all right." He wasn't about to let his girls down.

His friend since college, also his lawyer, Sam, walked up to the booth. "Well, hello, little darlin'."

Addy grinned. "Sam!" She reached out her arms and he picked her up.

"How's my favorite girl?" he asked.

"Good. I have a new friend at school." She frowned. "Please don't make me go stay with Grandpa Ben again."

He shook his head. "No way. You're going to go home with your daddy today."

That produced a big grin from the child. Sam looked at Laurel. "It's good to see you again, Laurel."

"Good to see you, too, Sam," Laurel said. "I hope this is the last time here at the courthouse."

He winked at her. "Thanks to you, I'm pretty sure this will be." He looked at Kase. "You ready to bring down the bad guy?"

RIGHT AT NOON, Sam and Kase stepped off the elevator onto the floor of Chappell, Hannett and Caruthers, Attorneys at Law. Kase paused and looked around the prestigious law offices. The dark paneling, light-hued walls, plush carpeting and offices with names gold embossed on the glass doors.

At the large reception desk, the pretty blonde looked up. Slowly her smile faded. "Oh, Mr. Rawlins."

"Hello, Jennifer."

She seemed to be at a loss as to what to say. Sam

stepped in. "We're here to see Ben Chappell and Charles Hannett. We have an appointment."

Jennifer quickly glanced at her computer screen. "Yes, of course, Mr. Gerrard. They are expecting you in conference room one. Please follow me." She took them down the hall. Kase knew where to go but let the woman do her job.

Jennifer knocked, then opened the door and announced them.

Letting his lawyer take the lead, Kase followed Sam inside to find Ben at the head of the table and Charles seated next to him.

Ben glared at him. "I told Charles I didn't want this meeting. You coming here was the only way I'd agree to it." He glared at Kase. "So get on with it. Are you willing to end this court battle over Addy?"

"Never," Kase said and sat down.

"Then there isn't anything else to discuss." Ben stood. "Come, Charles, they're wasting our time."

They had reached the door when Sam said, "I think you'll be interested, since it's about Addy's trust fund. Or we can save it for the judge."

Ben swung around, his face red with anger. "You can't have access to her funds. Her grandmother set that account up when Addy was born. I'm her trust officer."

"That's what we're here to talk about," Sam said. "This hasn't been a matter for the courts. Yet. I thought I'd give you the opportunity to keep the matter…private. Just between you and Kase. I'm sure you want to think about your granddaughter's best interest."

Charles spoke up. "Ben won't discuss anything without his lawyer present."

Sam grinned. "That's fine with me." He opened his

briefcase and took out the manila folder. "We have records from Addy's trust account."

"Stop!" Ben turned to his law partner. "Charles, I can handle this."

The distinguished older gentleman frowned. "No, Ben, I can't allow you to talk with them without representation."

Kase knew his father-in-law didn't want anyone to know about the disappearance of funds. Ben raised a hand to his law partner. "I said, I'll handle it, Charles. Please leave us."

"I advise against this, Ben. But I'll go." He walked out and closed the door behind him.

Ben glared at Kase. "How dare you go into Addy's trust."

Kase wasn't going to let this man intimidate him any longer. "Sit down, Ben. It's time you listened."

Seconds passed as if the man was weighing his options, but they all knew he had none. Ben pulled out the chair and sat down. Sam slid the portfolio across the table for Ben to see.

Ben shook his head. "I already know what's in the file."

Kase sat across from the man who'd given him a chance to build a career. He was to be the firm's golden boy. He wondered if the marriage to Johanna had been part of the program. He didn't care about that, because he got Addy. She was the reason he was here.

"Not much left for your granddaughter, is there?"

Ben continued his arrogant attitude. "She'll have plenty from her grandmother. Hell, Judith is loaded."

"Then why take from Addy?"

"It was just easier. Besides, I'm planning to pay it back."

"Damn, Ben," Kase began, "as a lawyer you knew you were breaking the law."

Ben's hand hit the high-gloss table. "Do you have any idea how much work it is to keep this practice going? How many clients it takes?"

Kase couldn't feel sorry for Ben. "Maybe when you started losing revenue, you should have downsized the practice." He glanced around. "You could have made a good living without all the fringe benefits."

Ben sent him a long hard stare. "I don't need a lecture from you. I made you. I gave you opportunity. You couldn't even handle my daughter, or the exclusive clients that I sent your way."

A few years ago, Ben's reprimand would have bothered him, but not anymore. "I cannot care less about the clients, but I'll regret not being able to help Johanna. Now Addy is without a mother."

"Johanna was always a headstrong child," Ben said. "She'd been a trial from the beginning."

Kase shook his head. Good Lord. Didn't this man have any paternal feelings?

Kase couldn't take any more. "Well, I can't do anything about the past, but I sure as hell can see that my daughter's future is secure."

"So sending her grandfather to jail will do that?"

"Don't make me out to be the bad guy," Kase said. "You tried to take my little girl away from me. If I thought that you loved her and it was in her best interest, I could understand. But this was purely for greed."

Ben looked defeated. "So now I lose my practice and get disbarred?"

Sam stepped in and began to speak. "Not necessarily. Although I advised him not to, Kase is willing to give you a second chance." His lawyer slid a paper across the table. "You sign this and give up this fight to take Addy. You have two years to pay back the money you stole from your granddaughter's trust," Sam said. "Also, make me the trustee of the account, or Kase, and no one will have to know about this."

Again, Ben hesitated.

Kase had had about enough. "You're not going to win this, Ben, not once I tell Judge Steffen you're embezzling Addy's money. Whether he is a friend or not, he can't overlook this. I win custody, and you don't go to jail."

"Take the offer, Ben," Sam encouraged. "It's more than you deserve."

It HAD TAKEN nearly two more hours before Sam and Kase finalized the details of the contract. The court also had to be notified the Chappells were dropping the custody case. Once they'd walked out of the conference room, everything was signed, sealed and notarized, then Sam took possession for safekeeping.

Kase couldn't wait to get back to his daughter and Laurel. Earlier, he'd gotten a message from Laurel saying she'd taken Addy to the aquarium.

He couldn't wait to see them. "I can't thank you enough for helping me," Kase told Sam as they climbed into a taxi. "You helped more than just representing me."

Sam grinned. "All right, I'll bill you extra for all those late-night calls."

They both laughed. "Go ahead. Today's results are worth everything. Name your price. How do you feel about a new foal?" He thought about the future horse that he shared with Laurel.

"I'll pass on the foal. There's a no-pet clause in my lease. But I wouldn't mind if you'd listen to a proposition I have."

Kase studied his friend's suddenly serious expression. "Okay."

"I have this venture I've been thinking about and I want to include you. How would you feel about practicing law again?"

FEELING BOTH EXCITED and anxious, Laurel kept a look-out for Kase as she walked Addy out of the Downtown Aquarium. He'd texted that he was on his way. After two hours of looking at sea creatures, even the mermaid show hadn't distracted the child. She wanted her father.

Kase hadn't been able to tell her much, only that he'd explain things when he got there. Why couldn't she get her heart to slow to a normal pace? Ever since Kase Rawlins had come back into her life, nothing had been calm and soothing.

She missed the days when she worked hard all day, and fell into bed at night exhausted from working her horses. Now she wanted to be with Kase and Addy. She wanted nothing more than to be a part of their lives.

Addy tugged on her arm. "Laurel, do you think the judge put Daddy in jail?"

She knelt down. "Oh, no, honey. Your daddy didn't do anything wrong. He just wants to make sure you get to stay with him." She put on a smile. "Just wait. He'll be here."

No sooner than she said the words, she heard her name called. She looked up and saw Sam and Kase rushing toward them. Her heart started racing. "See, Addy, I told you your daddy would be here."

The little girl took off and threw herself into Kase's arms. She watched the emotions play out on his face as he held his daughter close. He finally looked at Laurel. When his gaze locked on hers, she felt her body warm.

The need for this man was overwhelming. He set Addy down and he and Laurel walked toward each other.

He pulled her close and brushed his mouth over hers. "It's over, Laurel," he breathed. "I have permanent custody of Addy."

She released a breath. "Thank God."

"Thank you for all you did, too."

"I couldn't let Ben take your daughter. I know a little bit about being separated from family." She couldn't help but think about Brooke. She'd never gotten to know her twin until last year. "Addy needs you." She wanted to add, *I need you, too.*

"Why don't we go have a late lunch and celebrate? Then we can head home."

She loved the sound of that. "I'd like nothing more."

"Me, too," Addy cheered.

Kase turned to his friend. "Sam, come with us."

Sam shook his head. "Sorry. As much as I'd like to, I have another client to see today. I only wanted to say goodbye to Addy." He hugged the girl, then turned to Laurel and embraced her, too. "I hope I get the chance to know you better. I've heard so much about how great you are at training quarter horses."

She was touched that Kase had talked about her. "You're welcome on the Bucking Q anytime."

"I just might show up one day." He turned back to Kase. "Don't wait until you get into trouble to call me." He shook his hand and turned serious. "And think about my offer. You're too good a lawyer not to think about practicing law again."

Laurel froze. Practice law? A sudden ache settled in her stomach. Kase was thinking about going back to Denver?

Chapter Seventeen

Since returning from Denver two days ago, Laurel had been working from sunrise to sunset with her horses. She hadn't realized how much time she'd spent away from her normal routine until she climbed back in the saddle. She had Chet to thank for his help. And since she hadn't been called in at the accounting office, she could concentrate on doing her real job.

She missed the time she'd gotten to spend with Addy. But the child was in school most days, and Kase was busy doing his thing.

Did that include thinking about going back to practicing law? She didn't know. On their ride home from Denver, she'd hoped he might say something about Sam's offer. But not a word.

She'd gotten a call from him yesterday. He'd invited her to the house for dinner, saying he wanted to thank her for all she'd done for them.

She needed some time and space to think about his possible return to Denver. She'd turned down the invitation, saying she needed to put in extra training time with Ruby. This morning, the local florist arrived with a large spring bouquet, with a card that read "Thank you for everything you did. You're so special to us. Love, Kase and Addy."

LAUREL SAT UP on the large roan mare, going through the reining movements, starting with the circles, then she rode around the arena and into the flying lead change, the rundown and sliding stop. After Ruby backed up in a perfectly straight line, Laurel praised her.

"My good girl." She rubbed the mare's neck and repeated, "Such a good girl."

She heard cheers and looked over to the corral fence to see her sister. Laurel rode over to Brooke.

"Hey, what are you doing here?"

"Dad-and-daughters night, remember? We haven't gone out since before Chris was born."

She'd forgotten completely. "Speaking of my nephew, where is he?"

Brooke laughed. "Hey, doesn't anyone want to see me anymore?"

"Sorry, how are you doing?"

"I'm fine. Chris has been sleeping longer, so I'm getting more rest."

"You look great," Laurel said, amazed how Brooke managed to get into a pair of jeans when her baby was barely a month old.

"I'm eating like a horse. Breast feeding makes me so hungry." A big smile appeared. "But I love having that special connection with my baby."

Laurel felt tears threatening. What was wrong with her? She hated being envious of her sister because she had a husband…and a child. "You're so lucky," she told her and climbed down from Ruby. Brooke hadn't had an easy life. "You deserve it all."

"I count my blessings every day." Her sister studied her a moment. "Now, tell me what's bothering you."

Ruby was getting restless and Laurel called to Calvin, the new ranch hand. After Laurel's care instructions, he took the mare into the barn. "Just a little tired, I guess," she admitted. "I've been pretty busy."

Brooke waited until Laurel walked through the corral gate. It was true she hadn't known her twin long. In fact, it hadn't been a year yet since she came to the Bucking Q to meet Laurel.

"I know we're still new at being sisters, Laurel, but you can tell me anything. I won't even share with Trent."

Laurel made a face. "As much as I love that guy, he can be a little overprotective."

Brooke smiled. That was one of the many things she loved about her husband. "That's because Trent loves you."

"Yeah, he's the brother I never had," Laurel said.

Brooke frowned. "You don't think of Kase that way."

Laurel glanced away.

Brooke continued to prod. "I thought you'd be happy that Kase won the custody suit."

"I am. He never should have had to go through this."

"Then what's the problem? You two were getting pretty close, right? From where I stand, it looks like the man is crazy about you. Did you fight?"

"No. I just need to catch up with some training."

Brooke didn't like this. "What could be more important than being with the man you love? I seem to remember a certain sister who wouldn't let me give up on Trent."

They started walking toward the house. "That was different."

"How so? Have you talked with Kase about how you feel?"

Laurel stopped at the back door. "Look, Brooke, I think Kase is moving back to Denver." She went on to explain about Sam's job offer.

"Whoa, just because someone offered Kase a job

doesn't mean he's going to take it. Gus is here, and Addy is settled into school."

"Yeah, but Kase couldn't leave fast enough ten years ago. Maybe he's tired of small-town living again."

KASE WASN'T IN the mood to go out to dinner tonight. Not without Laurel anyway. But when he talked to her this morning, she let him know how busy she'd be the next few days. He hated that he'd taken so much of her time, so he let it go.

He looked down at his daughter. He saw how much more relaxed the child had been since coming back from Denver.

Now they could all move on, plan their lives, their futures. He only needed to convince Laurel.

They walked into the noisy atmosphere at Joe's Barbecue Smokehouse. Even for the middle of the week the place was crowded.

"Daddy!" His daughter tugged on his arm. "Look, Laurel's here. So is Pops and Brooke. I'm gonna go see them."

As usual, Addy took off running toward the table. He paused, seeing Laurel's big smile at Addy's arrival. Her arms went around his child and pulled her close, then the rest of the Quinns hugged her. That was what he wanted for his child. A family.

Gus came up to him. "You might want to avoid Laurel, but your daughter isn't going to let you."

"I'm not avoiding her. She's just busy."

"Don't give up, son." The older man shook his head.

Kase suddenly became determined. "I don't plan on it. Come on, we're crashing a family dinner."

"That's my boy."

Kase led the way and was ready to give Laurel a small

piece of his mind when she turned to him. Her smile wavered, and her eyes filled. What was going on here?

"Hello, Kase."

"Hello, Laurel." He leaned down and kissed her on the mouth, lingering a little longer than for just a friendly kiss. "I've missed you," he whispered.

Before she could answer, he looked around the table. "Good to see you, Rory." The men shook hands, then he turned to Laurel's sister. "Brooke, you look wonderful. Motherhood agrees with you."

"Thank you."

"Daddy, Brooke didn't bring Christopher with her because it's a princess party."

Brooke answered, "That's because Chris needs to be in bed. If Trent is lucky, our son is sound asleep by now."

Gus was chatting with Rory when the waitress showed up and asked, "Will they be joining you?"

"Of course," Rory said. "Please, join us for supper."

Kase looked right at Laurel. "Thank you, we'd like that." He got Addy situated next to Brooke and he took the chair beside Laurel. The waitress took their orders, and when the beers came, the conversation got interesting.

"I heard about your trip to Denver," Rory said. "Glad things worked out." He raised his beer. "To having your daughter where she belongs."

"I'll drink to that," Kase said, feeling Laurel's thigh brush his. He got a little distracted but worked to refocus. "It's thanks to your daughter, Rory. Let's say she stumbled onto some information that helped the case."

Addy looked up at her dad. "Laurel helped me so I didn't have to go live with Grandpa Ben. He doesn't have any horsies like Papa Gus. And soon, I'm getting my own pony when I'm five years old." She held up her fingers. "How soon is that, Daddy?"

"Your birthday is this summer, in July."

"Oh, yeah. On fireworks day."

Everyone laughed, and Rory said, "Why am I not surprised? You are a little firecracker."

Addy's eyes rounded. "Maybe that's what I can call my pony."

Under the table, Kase took hold of Laurel's hand and squeezed it. She finally turned and smiled at him. "I want to see you," he said, his voice low.

"I'm pretty busy, Kase. I have an early morning."

He shook his head. "I'll be over tonight."

Two hours later, Laurel paced her apartment. She wasn't ready to talk to Kase. She needed some more time. Maybe he wasn't going to return to Denver, but everything in her gut told her he would leave Hidden Springs. He was a top-notch lawyer who spent a lot of years in school to get his degree. And now that Addy's trust had been depleted of funds, maybe he felt he needed to make a larger income.

There was a knock on the door. She released a breath and went to answer it. A thrill raced through her seeing Kase standing there. Smiling, he stepped forward, pulled her into his arms. "I need this more than my next breath."

His mouth covered hers in a kiss that started out slow and easy but quickly began building her hunger. He parted her lips and she groaned as he slipped inside and tasted her.

Her arms found their way around his neck, and she tilted her head so he could deepen the kiss.

Kase finally pulled back, placing his forehead against hers. "I need you so much, Laurel." He kissed her again, then again. He finally picked her up and carried her to the bed.

She was weak when it came to this man, and she couldn't resist him. She needed him, too.

He laid her down on the mattress. She reached up to him. "Make love to me, Kase."

"I plan to," he said. He joined her, and she pushed aside the rest of the world and her problems for a little while. All that was important was loving Kase.

KASE PULLED LAUREL CLOSER. Why was he so afraid he was losing her? Ever since they left Denver, she'd been distant. Even making love, she held back from him.

He rolled over and looked down at her. "Look, Laurel, I didn't mean to walk in here and practically attack you."

She forced a smile. "I seemed to be a willing participant."

"What I wanted to do tonight was talk and find out what is wrong."

"I told you, nothing. I just have a lot of catching up to do. I've decided to ride Ruby Ridge in the Summer Slide Futurity in July."

He grinned. "That's wonderful. I'm so proud of you for following through on this new venture."

She shrugged. "I know I'm a good trainer, but I also have a great horse. I've been lucky with Ruby. Now, Wind I'm not so sure of."

He kissed her lips. "It's not that I don't want to hear about your horses, but another time. This is you-and-me time. I want to talk about the future."

She sat up on the bed, then reached for his shirt off the floor and slipped it on. "Maybe it's not a good idea right now."

"Why? Things are settled with Addy."

"But they aren't resolved with Jack, and the money I owe my dad and Trent." She shook her head. "We can't think about anything right now. Besides, you aren't ready."

He got up, too, grabbed his jeans and slipped them on. Walking to the window, he turned her around. "Who says I'm not ready?"

"I do. You haven't been home long enough to know what you want."

Kase stood back and folded his arms across his chest. "Really? You don't believe that I came home to make a life here?"

"You left before, Kase. You're a big-time lawyer who's lived a pretty exciting life. In ten years, you achieved a lot in Denver. I don't blame you for wanting to go back. You had a beautiful home, money and a law practice. Not everyone is cut out for small-town living."

Did she really think he wanted his old life back? "What suddenly brought this on?"

She shrugged. "I overheard Sam offer you a job."

She must not have heard all of the conversation. "So you just assume that I'm going back to Denver?"

She looked at him. "You tell me, Kase. Are you moving back?"

Kase was angry. How could she think that he'd just pick up and leave her? Maybe because he'd done it before. "Laurel…"

Her cell phone suddenly went off. She went to the table and picked it up. "Oh, no, it's the same number from before," she told him. "Jack…"

Kase went to her side. "Answer it on Speaker, and if he asks why, tell him you're in the car."

Laurel was shaky when she finally pressed the button. "Jack?"

"Sorry, Laurel, but I had to talk to you again." His words were slurred. "I'm leaving for a long…long time."

"He's been drinking," she mouthed. Kase motioned for her to keep him talking.

"Where are you going, Jack?"

"Doesn't matter," Jack said. "I just wanted to tell you…I'm so sorry, Laurel. Sweet Laurel. I shouldn't have ever taken the money. So I'm gonna give it back."

Kase signaled for her to keep talking. "Really, Jack? Why should I believe you?"

"Because, dammit! I never wanted to steal it, but people were threatening me."

"What about me, Jack? I was going to be your wife, or was I part of the ruse, too?"

There was a long pause and he finally said, "Leaving you was the hardest part, Laurel. But everything fell apart. I had no choice."

Before Laurel could think of anything to say, Jack announced, "I want to see you, Laurel, before I go away. I promise I won't bother you ever again. I'll be at the Branding Iron, in the parking lot until twelve o'clock. If you don't come, I'll understand."

Before she could answer, Jack hung up.

Kase punched in a number. "Yes, Sheriff. Laurel heard from Aldrich." He turned away and gave the information to the officer.

Laurel grabbed her clothes and began putting them on. She slipped on her boots, and by the time Kase was off the phone, she was out the door.

"Laurel," Kase said as he caught her at the base of the steps. "You can't go there. It isn't safe."

"He won't hurt me. Besides, I'm the reason the money was taken in the first place."

"No, you're not. Jack knew how to work his victims."

"There aren't going to be any more victims if I can help it."

He held her hand tight. "Don't go, Laurel. This man is on the run. That means he's dangerous."

Kase pulled her close and buried his face in her hair. "I can't lose you again, Laurel." His heart was beating hard and fast. "It would kill me."

She raised her head to look at him. "Oh, Kase. You aren't going to lose me."

"Then stay here, Laurel. The sheriff will get Jack. No amount of money is worth the risk."

He placed his finger over her lips to stop her argument. "You are too important to me. It's just taken me ten years to realize that. All I ask is a chance to prove it."

Chapter Eighteen

With help from her parents, Kase managed to keep Laurel from leaving. So for the next two hours, a sullen Laurel sat in the Quinns' kitchen, ignoring him as they all waited for news. The only information they'd gotten about Aldrich had been nothing but sketchy. So all they could do was let law enforcement handle it.

He got up and walked to the back door. Rory followed him. "If you haven't noticed, Laurel has inherited the Quinn stubbornness."

Kase glanced back at him. "Throw in a little pride and a lot of determination, and disregard for her safety." He ran his hand through his hair. "Do you know she's hell-bent on paying you back the money Jack stole?"

Rory nodded. "Trent and I haven't been able to convince her that she's not responsible. Hell, we hired Aldrich. Even without Laurel, the man would have figured out how to hack into our account."

Kase released a breath. "Somehow we have to resolve this, because Laurel isn't going to let it go." Dammit, she deserved to be free of the jerk.

Suddenly headlights appeared and Kase rushed out as he recognized the sheriff's vehicle. Rory and Laurel followed close behind to meet the fifty-five-year-old sheriff, Ted Carson, as he climbed out of the patrol car.

"Hello, Rory, Laurel. Kase."

"Sheriff," Kase greeted him. "Please tell me you have some good news."

He nodded. "We apprehended Jack Aldrich. He's in custody at the jail."

"Thank God," Rory said. "Do you need us to press charges?"

"Yes, but it can wait until tomorrow. I just wanted to come out to ease your mind." He looked at Laurel. "Would you mind answering some questions tomorrow, too?"

"Sure. Could you tell me if there was any money found on him?" Laurel asked.

Ted paused, then said, "About five thousand, but that's evidence right now."

Kase suddenly went into lawyer mode. "I'll be with her tomorrow, Sheriff."

"I have nothing to hide, Kase."

"I didn't say you did, but it doesn't hurt to have someone with you." Kase looked at the sheriff. "We'll be there in the morning."

Ted Carson nodded. "Then I'll expect you in my office at nine o'clock." He walked back to his car and drove off.

"I didn't think about us having to press charges," Laurel said.

"Trent and your father were the ones who reported the theft to the sheriff last year," Kase said. "And, of course, the bank is concerned they allowed an unauthorized person access to the account."

"No, I'm the reason Jack got my user ID and password," Laurel announced. "I'm sorry, Dad. If I hadn't been so careless..."

"Stop it," Rory said. "We all trusted Jack. And after tomorrow we can finally move on and forget that bastard."

"But what about the money?"

Rory shook his head. "The money has been replaced, then Trent got a new loan, the cabins were completed and they're renting. End of story. Now, I think we can all use some sleep. Good night." He kissed his daughter, then walked back into the house.

"Come on, Laurel. You need sleep, too." Kase took her hand and started toward the garage. The stone pathway was well lit, as were the wooden stairs that led up to her second-floor apartment. He hated that he had to leave her now, but he needed to get home to Addy.

"It's okay, Laurel. Jack is going to jail. He isn't going to bother you again." Kase pulled her into his arms. "This isn't how I wanted to spend tonight, but there's plenty of time to talk now that everything is settled with Aldrich."

Why didn't he feel as convinced as his words? And after one look at Laurel, he knew she wasn't giving him any encouragement, either.

THE NEXT MORNING, Kase dropped Addy off at school, then he headed over to the sheriff's office on Main Street. He saw the familiar truck parked at the curb and inside were Rory, Trent and Laurel.

Laurel was dressed in her standard working clothes, jeans, a Henley shirt and boots. He happened to like that look.

Rory greeted him and he glanced at the sheriff, not happy that they'd all spoken without legal representation. "Have you already questioned them?"

Ted frowned. "It wasn't an interrogation, Counselor. Just some basic questions about what happened. Now we're finished, and I'll be taking the prisoner to the courthouse to be arraigned and formally charged."

Kase nodded and looked over their statements. Everything seemed to be in order. He looked at Laurel. "You okay?"

She put on a smile. "Yeah. Since Jack confessed to the crime, we don't even have to testify."

Kase was happy about that. "Good. How about I take you all out to breakfast?"

Trent stepped up and said, "I'd like to, but I have to get packed for a fishing trip early tomorrow."

Rory excused himself, too.

Kase looked back at Laurel. "Looks like it's you and me."

"They're my ride, Kase." She started to leave, but he stopped her.

"Laurel, at least let me drive you home. I'd like to finish our discussion from last night."

She turned away from her father and Trent. "I can't do this right now, Kase," she said, her voice low. "Besides, you have to think about what you really want, too. For both you and Addy." She turned and walked out the door.

Kase started to follow her, but stopped. What good would it do? She wasn't ready to listen to anything he had to say. He could be stubborn, too.

He looked at Rory. "I'm not going to give up. I love your daughter."

Rory arched an eyebrow. "I'm not the one you have to convince, son. Laurel's been hurt more than she lets on. It might take a while."

"I'm not going anywhere."

THREE DAYS LATER, Laurel received a bouquet of roses along with a handwritten invitation to dinner with Kase and Addy. The little girl even printed her own name and said to dress as a princess. And a chariot would pick her up at six o'clock. Laurel smiled and frantically searched her closet until she found a suitable dress, one she'd worn in a friend's wedding.

With one last look in the mirror, Laurel was happy with her reflection. The pink satin gown had a fitted bodice and off-the-shoulders sleeves. The tea length showed off a pair of strappy sandals. She wore her hair down in curls. She told herself she was doing this for Addy, but she couldn't wait to see Kase's expression.

Her father came up the stairs. "I believe your prince has arrived."

If possible, Laurel's heart raced harder. She glanced at her mother.

"Don't think so hard, Laurel," Diane told her. "Just listen to your heart and to a man who loves you."

"I tried that before and it didn't work."

"Forget about the past." She nodded toward the door. "Your prince awaits."

"I know, but can I trust him?"

Diane exchanged a special look with her husband. "Sometimes even the best princes make mistakes, but when they come back to you, that's when you know that it's meant to be."

Laurel knew that her mother was talking about the time before she and Rory were married. They broke up, and that was when Rory met Coralee during the rodeo finals. Then realizing his mistake, he'd come back to the woman he truly loved.

Laurel kissed her parents, accepted a shawl from her mother, then walked out to find Kase standing at the bottom of the stairs.

He was dressed in a fitted black tux and a white pleated shirt and bow tie. He was one gorgeous man. In his hand he held a long-stem red rose.

His silver gaze never left her. "You look incredibly beautiful." He took hold of her hand, then kissed it.

Laurel took the rose he offered her and inhaled the floral scent. "You look handsome, too," she managed to say.

"You have no idea how much I want to kiss you right now, but if I do, I won't be able to stop." He released a shuddered breath and said, "And I promised Addy I'd bring you to the house."

Laurel nodded, discovering she was a little excited to see what he had planned for her. "Then we should get going."

The limo driver held the door as Kase helped her into the vehicle. She relaxed against the plush leather seat as Kase opened a bottle of champagne, then poured her a glass.

She accepted the flute. "This is so fancy."

"I hope to impress you tonight."

He'd been doing that ever since returning from Denver. She took a sip, enjoying the bubbly drink. "It's not that hard. I've been impressed with you since I was a freshman in high school." Oh, God. Did she really say that out loud?

He turned to her, showing off that sexy grin that made her body tingle. Suddenly she wished they could keep driving away from all their troubles and distractions.

He touched his glass to hers, then he took a drink and said, "The first time I noticed you, I mean really noticed you, you had on this pretty blue-green sweater and a pair of dark jeans. Your hair was pulled back and nearly hung to your waist. The last bell had just rung and I walked out of the building and saw you waiting for the school bus. It was like a lightning bolt hit me, and it took me a week before I got the nerve to talk to you."

She blinked. He'd remembered? She took a hearty sip of courage. "Do we need to go through this?"

"I do, Laurel." He took her hand and pressed it against his thigh. "We were just kids back then, but I knew what I wanted. You." He touched her chin and made her look at him. "But I was a selfish kid who had something to prove. I pretty much got everything I wished for, then realized I didn't have the right person to share it with." His voice lowered. "You're what I want, Laurel. I don't think I ever stopped wanting you."

"Oh, Kase. I never stopped wanting you, either. But we're not those kids any longer. So much has happened..."

He stopped her protest when his mouth covered hers. She couldn't think then, could only feel the intoxicating rush that went through her with his look or touch. She reached around and combed her fingers into his hair. She moaned as he deepened the kiss, slipping his tongue past her lips and tasting her.

He tore his mouth away, breathing hard. "Whoa, we'd better slow down." He pressed his head against hers as the limo came to a stop. "We'll have to continue this later. It's time for a party."

Kase climbed out, happy the evening air was cool. He took a breath and released it, then reached in and helped Laurel out.

Offering her his arm, he escorted her to the front of the Rawlinses' home. When they reached the porch, the door opened and Gus appeared with a smile. Addy had managed to talk him into wearing a tux this evening, as well. Kase loved his father for playing along.

"Good evening, Princess Laurel. You look especially beautiful tonight."

"Thank you, Prince Gus," she returned. "You look mighty handsome yourself."

Gus bowed. "Princess Addy is waiting for you in the parlor."

The Rawlins home wasn't large, but there was a small entry that opened into a large living area with a used brick fireplace as the centerpiece. Kase had many improvement plans for his childhood home. But first, he had to convince Laurel to share his life.

The lights had been dimmed, but there was the addition of candlelight. Addy stood in the middle of the room in a long pink princess dress he'd bought in town. He'd also added some sparkly bows to her hair.

"Hello, Addy," Laurel greeted. "Oh, my, don't you look pretty." She went over and bent down and hugged her. "Thank you for inviting me tonight."

Addy giggled. "I wanted to have a princess night like you do with your dad, but with us together." The child looked over Laurel's dress. "You look like a real princess, too." Her head full of curls bobbed. "Doesn't she, Daddy?"

"Yes, she does. You both are lovely." Kase reached in his pocket and took out his phone and took their picture.

Addy said, "Thank you for coming to my dinner."

"And thank you for sharing your princes with me."

Addy looked back at her dad. "Tonight, you can have Daddy as your prince, and I have Papa Gus as my prince."

Kase watched his daughter as she played her part as practiced. Gus came in and took his granddaughter's arm and walked her into the dining room. The table was draped in lace, long tapers sat in the center and there were four place settings. Gus helped Addy into her chair as Kase assisted Laurel.

Then both men went into the kitchen and came out with plates of spaghetti. Kase retrieved a basket of bread and set it on the table. "Addy chose the menu."

Laurel was generous with her praise toward his daughter. "It's one of my favorite meals."

Kase sat down at the end of the table with Laurel to his right. They said a short blessing and began to eat.

"This is really good," Laurel said. "You look so pretty I think next time you should talk your prince into going out to a restaurant."

Addy giggled. "I know, but this time we wanted to come here to celebrate my coming home for good. Daddy said I never have to go back to Denver." She smiled. "I want to live here forever and ever. I pretend this is my castle." She twirled her spaghetti with her fork. "And Daddy is going to make it bigger."

"Really?"

Addy nodded. "He's going to build more rooms and fix the kitchen and make a bigger corral. Do you like that idea?"

"Well, that's a lot of work."

"Daddy and Papa Gus want to have more horses, too." The girl beamed. "And I need a stall for when I get my pony for my birthday."

"A princess with a pony." Laurel smiled and took a bite of her food. "What else do you want for your birthday?"

Kase sat back, hoping his daughter wouldn't give away too much. Addy shot a look at him and he placed a finger against his mouth. "Oh, it's a secret."

Laurel took another bite of her food. After swallowing, she said, "So, you've decided to do some remodeling."

"It's time," he told her, knowing Gus wouldn't give in if it weren't for the fact his granddaughter asked him. "And I got Dad to agree."

Gus shrugged. "I didn't have much choice. The family is expanding."

"Shh, Papa," Addy whispered. "It's a secret."

"What secret?" Laurel asked again.

Kase smiled. "We'll tell you after dinner."

ABOUT THIRTY MINUTES later the meal concluded with dishes of ice cream with chocolate sauce. Then the men carried the dirty dishes into the kitchen.

Laurel still hadn't learned any more about what was really going on, especially when Addy got down from the table and announced it was bedtime. After Addy gave Laurel a hug, Gus walked his little princess up the stairs to bed.

Laurel turned and looked at Kase. "Okay, what's going on?"

He gave her an innocent shrug. "I wanted some alone time with you."

Remembering the kiss in the car, she wasn't sure if she could handle another. Kase had a way of making her forget her common sense. He crossed the room toward her, and his heated gaze left no denying his desire for her. She wanted this man, too.

He took her hand and said, "Come with me. I have something to show you."

With her nod they walked down the hall to the office. On the old desk was a set of architectural plans spread across the top.

"I had plans drawn up for an addition to the house." He pointed to the French doors behind them. "They're going to blow out the entire back of the house and add another suite of rooms. There will be two rooms with another bathroom downstairs, and a large master suite with a bath upstairs. The kitchen will be remodeled, adding space from part of the mudroom."

Laurel's head was spinning. "This is a big project."

"It's going to be Addy's and my home." He removed

his tux jacket and draped it over her shoulders. "Come on, I'll show you." He opened the French doors and they stepped out to a small deck. The sun was setting, and there was a gold-and-orange hue outlining the mountains. The land was dense with giant pine trees. The scene stole her breath.

She leaned against the railing. "It's beautiful here."

He stood beside her. "It's the reason I wanted the bedrooms on the backside of the house with a wall of windows." He sighed. "Can you imagine waking up to this view?"

She would love nothing more. "It would be heavenly."

He turned to face her. The light was growing dim, but she could still see his incredible eyes. He touched her face. "Yes, it would, but only if you're with me."

Her heart was pounding. "Oh, Kase…"

"Hear me out." He brushed a soft kiss across her lips. "I love you, Laurel. I don't think I ever stopped. It's just taken me years to wise up and realize what's important. You. You are so important to me, and my family. I want to build a life here with you, Addy and Gus."

She didn't get a chance to answer as his mouth closed over hers. Suddenly she lost the fight and wrapped her arms around him and gave in to the feelings.

Kase broke off the kiss. "Sorry, you got me a little distracted." He kissed her nose. "Now, where was I?"

She had no idea. "Something about building a life together."

He smiled. "So toss out any doubts you have, and I bet I have a solution."

"This isn't funny, Kase."

"No, it's serious. I want you in my life, Laurel. I know you hate the fact that your family lost money, and nothing I say will convince you that you aren't to blame. And there's nothing I can do to get that money back, but I have an idea on how to replace it."

She frowned. "Okay, I'm listening."

He grew serious. "The first idea is we could invest in Q and L Rental Cabins. Help your dad expand the business."

"I won't take any money from you," she argued.

"No, not from me, but from us. We have the foal. The money we get from selling the horse, we can invest in the rental cabins. And any profits we make, we give to Trent and Rory until all the money is paid back." He paused, then went on. "After talking with both your father and Trent, they'll only accept ten thousand. That's one-third of the money because they feel they should pay, too."

Laurel was stunned to say the least. "You'd sell your foal?"

He nodded. "Rory and Trent are already drawing up plans for phase two of the cabins. Brooke thinks we should concentrate on weddings and also cater to families, maybe think about adding horseback riding."

"Seems you've been busy."

"Of course, this is our future. I don't want to lose you, Laurel, especially over money."

She was touched and thrilled. "You never lost me, Kase." But she was still reluctant. "What happens when Hidden Springs isn't enough? When I'm not enough?" Her voice began to fade away. "Sam offered you a job, and I can't compete with that."

He reached for her. "Ah, baby, this isn't a competition. Sam's job offer was so I could stay here with Addy, Dad and you. The job offer from Sam was to do legal consulting online." He blew out a breath. "I nearly lost my daughter, Laurel, and I never want another parent to go through that. I want to help fathers who feel they don't have any rights."

She felt tears well in her eyes. "Oh, Kase. You'd be wonderful at that."

"So you like the idea?"

She nodded. "Very much."

He cupped her face tenderly. "Good, because I love you, Laurel Quinn. And I want us to work this time."

She nodded. "And I love you, Kase Rawlins."

"The sweetest words I could ever hear. Hold that thought." He reached into the pocket of his jacket she was wearing and pulled out a velvet box.

Laurel gasped when he opened the lid and she saw an incredible platinum ring with a pear-shaped emerald surrounded by small diamonds. "Oh, Kase."

"Addy helped me pick it out. So you like it?"

"Oh, yes, but I love you and Addy more. I don't need a ring."

He wasn't listening to her protest as he went down on one knee in front of her. "Addy instructed me on how a prince is to ask for your hand." He looked up at her, his expression serious. "Laurel Kathryn Quinn, I love you more than I could ever put into words, but over the next fifty years I'm going to do my best. Will you do me the honor of becoming my wife?"

"Oh, yes. Yes…yes…yes!"

He stood and slipped the ring on her finger, then kissed her until they were both breathless.

"I want nothing more than to carry you off to bed and make love to you, but I promised one little girl that she would be the first to know if you were going to be her mommy."

Laurel's chest tightened. "Oh, Kase. Do you think she'll be awake?"

"Let's go find out."

Like two kids, they hurried up the steps and quietly opened the child's door and silently walked inside to find Addy sound asleep.

"I think she's asleep," Kase said in a loud whisper. "We'll just tell her in the morning."

"Daddy! Laurel!" Addy sat up, rubbing her eyes. "Tell me what?"

Laurel sat down on the bed. "Sorry to wake you, sweetheart, but we wanted our daughter to be the first to know." She held out the beautiful ring.

"Oh, it's so sparkly." She smiled as she looked at Laurel. "Are you my mom now?"

Fighting tears, she pulled the child close. "Now and forever."

Kase sat down behind her. "And we're going to live happily ever after."

Laurel felt Kase's arms around her and she knew she found what she'd been looking for. It was definitely worth the wait.

Epilogue

The autumn leaves blew across the Rawlins Horse
Ranch's new corral. Laurel rode Wind around the arena,
taking him through his reining exercises. Over the past
four months, the wayward stallion had shown a lot of
promise. And she still trained Ruby Ridge, who made a
good showing in Laurel's first reining competition.

Even with the recent move from the Bucking Q to their
new home at the Rawlins Ranch a few days ago, both
horses had adjusted nicely. Wind seemed to be happy
sharing a barn with Honor's Promise. The mare was fat
and sassy like all pregnant moms should be.

A pang of envy hit Laurel. Her own desire was still
unfulfilled. Although she loved her new daughter, she
wanted a baby, Kase's baby.

Since her June wedding to Kase, they'd forgone
a honeymoon, but both wanted to add to the family.
Maybe now that all the construction on the house and
new arena was completed, they could concentrate on
each other. Warmth surged through her as her thoughts
turned to the sexy man who'd been curled up against
her this morning, eager to please her. His every touch,
his kisses…

A horn honked, startling Laurel back to reality, and
she saw Kase pull his SUV into the driveway. She felt

the excitement; her husband and daughter were home. Laurel climbed off Wind and handed the horse off to their new ranch hand, Charlie. She caught up with Gus as he came out of the barn.

"I guess we missed them today, huh?" She hugged her father-in-law. She knew he'd given up a lot with them all moving in together. He had a new suite of rooms on the ground floor with his own sitting room, bedroom and bath. He even had his own entrance, if he wanted more privacy.

"After all these years, this old cowboy loves having his family here."

She slipped her arm around his waist and together they walked to the car. "We're the ones who've been blessed, Gus. We need you around."

He nodded. "I just don't want you to feel I'm in your way."

"I love you being in my way."

They reached the car as Addy was getting out of the backseat. "Hi, Mommy."

Laurel's chest tightened hearing her new title. Addy decided on their wedding day that was what she wanted Laurel to be. Her father got a wife and she got a new mommy.

Addy hugged her. "We stopped at Pop Rory's house and saw the new cabins. And I got to ride Firecracker but just for a little bit. Daddy said when we bring my pony here, I can ride more."

"Yes, you can," Laurel told her. They hadn't been able to bring all the horses over yet. "Was Mimi there?"

"Yes, she gave me some cookies." She held out a plastic bag. "I have to save them for after lunch. She was going to see Coralee with Aunt Brooke. She said she would take me the next time."

It saddened Laurel that their biological mother's Alzheimer's had become a lot more aggressive in the past few months. The last time Laurel had visited her, the woman didn't know her. It was different for Brooke. Coralee had raised her and her twin was hurting over this loss. "We'll both go with Aunt Brooke the next time."

Gus stepped up. "And how about we go and start on lunch now?" He shuffled the child into the house.

Kase pulled his wife into his arms and relished the feel of her against him. "I missed you today." He kissed her, reminding him that just hours ago, they'd been making love in their new bedroom, in their new bed. "So much."

She laughed. "You were only gone four hours."

"It was *five* hours. Maybe I need to rethink this new career path."

"Oh, no, you don't. You're a wonderful lawyer, and Sam needs you."

His good friend Sam Gerrard had done what he promised and opened a small law office in Hidden Springs. Kase went to work in the mornings when he took Addy to school, and did consultations online.

He tossed her a sexy grin that had her body stirring to life. "You're right, I'm enjoying it. How was your morning?"

"It went well. Wind seems to be adjusting to his new home. I worked both him and Ruby pretty much the entire morning. I guess I'm a little tired."

"I don't know why. Besides training horses and being a new mother and a wife, you've supervised the remodel of the house. You've been going nonstop for months." He wrapped his arm across her shoulders and whispered against her ear. "Want to go take a nap?"

She arched an eyebrow. "Do you mean a nap, nap?"

He smiled. "We can see how tired you are when I get you upstairs."

He escorted Laurel through the mudroom, where she removed her boots. In the new kitchen there were pristine white cabinets and dark granite countertops with stainless-steel appliances, including the much-needed dishwasher. Instead of the old maple table, there was a large breakfast bar, where Addy sat eating her peanut butter and grape jelly sandwich.

"Laurel's going to take a nap. I'll change my clothes and be back down in a few minutes."

Laurel kissed the child on the head, then walked through the great room, then the new open staircase that led to the second floor. Together they walked toward the new section of the house, their sanctuary, the master suite.

Kase opened the double doors and followed his wife into the large ivory-carpeted room. Against one wall was a king-size bed covered in a plush burgundy comforter, adorned with navy and ivory pillows. The other wall was all windows, with a set of French doors that led out to a deck with that glorious mountain view.

Laurel walked to the bed, pulled back the covers and lay down. Concerned, he walked over immediately and sat down next to her.

"I felt fine this morning," she said.

He brushed wayward strands of hair from her flushed face. "How do you feel outside of being tired?"

She shrugged. "I'm not very hungry. Food kind of makes me sick to even think about."

Kase caught her pale coloring as she turned to her side. "Honey, I think you've worn yourself out with all the work going on around here."

He rubbed her back in slow, soothing circles.

"You worked hard, too." She took hold of his hand. "Sorry, I had plans for this afternoon. I thought we could go horseback riding. Pretty soon it will be too cold."

There was a knock on the door. "Come in," Kase called.

Brooke poked her head inside and smiled. "You two decent? I thought I'd stop by, since I was out with Chris." She walked in, then she frowned. "What's wrong?"

"I'm fine, really." Laurel sat up. "I guess I've been overdoing it."

Brooke eyed Kase. "Really. Huh, just a second." She went into their bath, then returned carrying a box. "I figured you had a few of these on hand." She gave it to her sister. "Maybe you should use it now." She started for the door. "I won't say a word until you call me with the news."

Laurel frowned, then looked at the pregnancy test. She glanced at Kase but couldn't speak. She'd taken the test before and it had come out negative.

She wanted to say that it was impossible to be pregnant, but she couldn't. She looked at her husband. "Don't say anything yet." She got up off the bed and went into the bathroom.

Nearly ten minutes later she returned to the bedroom. She handed the stick to her husband. "I don't think I can look."

"Laurel, I know how badly you want a baby, but we've only been trying for a few months."

"I know. And I get to adopt Addy." She walked into his arms. Everything always seemed better when Kase held her close. "I'm one lucky girl even if we never have a child."

"We're the lucky ones, Laurel. Addy and I have you. I love you so much."

She realized how much her life had changed in just a year. She almost married the wrong man. She discovered she had a different mother, and a twin sister. But most important, she found her way back to Kase. If she had anything to teach Addy, it was to make sure she held out for the right man.

"I love you, Kase Rawlins."

Kase captured her mouth and she immediately gave in to the heartwarming pleasure he gave her.

He tore his mouth away. "I think we need to see the results."

She nodded bravely, but her heart pounded in her chest. Was she ready for this? Disappointment. Or motherhood.

Kase eyed the stick, but his expression didn't give anything away.

"Okay, tell me," she begged.

He looked down at her, his silver gaze warm and loving. "I think we need to go downstairs and ask Addy if she wants a brother or a sister." A big grin appeared on his face.

"Oh, my God. Really, truly?"

He nodded and she saw the tears in his eyes. "I love you, Laurel. You've already given me and Addy so much." He placed his hand over her stomach. "And now this miracle…"

She laughed as her own happy tears spilled down her cheeks. "I guess from the day Wind found his way here, we've been destined to be parents."

He kissed her again. "Thank you for giving me a second chance."

"We were both given another chance." She wrapped her arms around his neck. "This time we're not wasting a moment of it."

* * * * *